THE DIVIDED HEART

Jean Morrant

CHIVERS
THORNDIKE

This Large Print book is published by BBC Audiobooks Ltd, Bath, England and by Thorndike Press®, Waterville, Maine, USA.

Published in 2006 in the U.K. by arrangement with the author.

Published in 2006 in the U.S. by arrangement with Jean Hall.

U.K. Hardcover ISBN 1–4056–3644–0 (Chivers Large Print)
ISBN 13: 978 1 405 63644 5
U.K. Softcover   ISBN 1–4056–3795–1 (Camden Large Print)
ISBN 13: 978 1 405 63795 4
U.S. Softcover   ISBN 0–7862–8737–3 (British Favorites)

The text of this Large Print edition is unabridged.
Other aspects of the book may vary from the original edition.

Set in 16 pt. New Times Roman.

Printed in Great Britain on acid-free paper.

British Library Cataloguing in Publication Data available

Library of Congress Cataloging-in-Publication Data

Morrant, Jean.
    The divided heart / by Jean Morrant.
       p.   cm.
    "Thorndike Press large print British favorites."
    ISBN 0–7862–8737–3 (pbk. : alk. paper)
    1. Sisters—Fiction. 2. Catalonia (Spain)—Fiction. 3. Large type books. I. Title.
    PR6113.O755D58 2006
    823'.92—dc22   2006010070

Books should be returned or renewed by the
last date stamped above.

00884\DTP\R N\04.05   LIB 7

CUSTOMER SERVICE EXCELLENCE

CHAPTER ONE

Following a bitter exchange with her sister, Garland McLeod left the family's holiday villa to walk briskly down the quiet street of the small Catalan town in the direction of Pedro's cafe situated at the end of the promenade. There, she could sit in the shade of a parasol and sip lemon tea, away from Sarah's conceited chatter and uncalled for advice which Garland attributed to the influence of her sister's glamorous friend, Patricia Blanford, and Don Meredith, wealthy owner of one of the most popular nightspots in Europe. It had been just the same today only, after last night's 'little incident', as Sarah casually referred to it, the need to escape was greater than ever.

So preoccupied was she with thoughts of that dreadful party the previous evening, the sudden blare of a horn didn't immediately register. It was the screech of brakes that brought her back to reality as she started to cross the road, colliding with the now stationary car.

'Dios!' came an angry exclamation from the open car window but, although aware she was at fault, she merely shot the driver a furious glance and hastened round the corner to reach the welcome safety of the little cafe.

Conscious of the rapid pounding of her heart, she paused and took a steadying breath. Usually she had more sense than to cross at that point and continued along the pavement to where the traffic was clearly visible. Not that there was much traffic—April was a quiet month—few tourists came to the coastal areas of north-east Spain so early in the year. But she had noticed an air of expectancy about the place; a distinct whiff of fresh paint, and an abundance of flowers cascading over the terracotta pots hanging from the whitewashed walls.

Selecting the usual table at the quiet end of the patio, Garland took one of the ornamental chairs. For the past week she had called at the café daily so now Pedro no longer came to take her order but appeared in the doorway wearing his same welcoming smile to which she merely nodded and settled back in her seat. For a moment she had considered ordering something stronger to steady her nerves until she recalled Don Meredith's behavior in his club the previous evening. Not that one drink was going to affect her the way Don had been affected—he'd had goodness knows how many—making him totally unreasonable when she refused his offer of employment as a driver. She held a driving licence, true, but she would require much more experience on these busy, unfamiliar roads to feel confident behind the wheel and cover the distances Don had stipulated. And after she reiterated her refusal, explaining that she was already employed in her father's sportswear business, he had turned on the charm when she'd had to reject his over friendly advances. Although Sarah hadn't actually heard Don's offensive taunts she excused his lapse as being due to his stressful business life, but Garland blamed his intake of alcohol for ruining her evening, and considered him a rather dubious character.

Uttering a soft groan of humiliation, she closed her eyes in an attempt to blot out the memory, only opening them at the sound of approaching footsteps. Expecting to see Pedro with her tray of tea, she started in surprise when she glanced up to find the driver of the vehicle she had only recently encountered towering arrogantly over her.

'*Senorita!* I trust you are unhurt . . .' he began, his slightly accented voice tinged with annoyance.

'Thank you, yes, I'm fine,' she broke in to assure him. 'A little shaken . . . nothing more.'

'Fortunately I have good brakes,' he continued, 'otherwise you could have been killed?'

'Y-yes I know, and I'm sorry . . .'

'Sorry!' he derided with an arrogant lift of his dark head. 'It was hardly the ideal place to cross. In future, I suggest you take more care.'

Becoming annoyed by his autocratic manner

she confirmed shortly, 'Don't worry, I will.'

'I do not wish you to come to any harm,' he said, his voice softening a little as he observed the flush of annoyance on her cheeks.

'I don't make a habit of it!' she returned, indignation sharpening her tone. 'Usually I keep to the pavement until I reach the Tropic Hotel opposite.'

'So I have noticed,' he responded quickly, a flicker of a smile playing round his firm mouth, and indicating the empty chair, enquired, 'May I join you?'

For a moment she hesitated then, intrigued by his last remark, nodded towards the vacant seat opposite. She couldn't recall seeing him here on previous visits, yet thought she detected a hint of recognition in Pedro's expression as he placed her tray on the table.

Draping his well-cut jacket over the back of the chair, the stranger seated himself, and when he also chose to order lemon tea, she noticed Pedro move off with a more purposeful stride.

'You were saying?' she queried, her eyes drawn to the stranger opposite as he removed his sunglasses and slid them into his pocket.

'Ah yes, what was I saying?' he asked after a moment, one dark brow raised mockingly as he held her gaze across the table.

'You mentioned you had noticed where I usually cross the road,' she prompted, assuring him quickly, 'Not that it's of any importance . . .'

He smiled, his dark eyes crinkling attractively at the corners. 'But you are curious—yes?'

She shrugged. 'Well, I don't recall seeing you here before.' Yet, now he had removed the dark glasses, she felt there was something faintly familiar about his face. Of course, it was quite possible he had used the remark merely to further their acquaintance. Even so, she had a curious feeling she'd seen him somewhere previously. That flick of dark hair falling onto a broad forehead, the slightly hooked nose, and an intriguing smile; all vaguely familiar.

'My very first visit to this cafe,' he told her, extending a well-manicured hand to draw attention to the hotel across the way. 'Each afternoon I have observed you taking tea at this table from a window opposite, but today you are a little earlier than usual.'

She cast him a rueful glance. 'Had I not been, you would have escaped that hair-raising experience on the road and observed me from a much safer distance—although it's rather disconcerting to find I've been spied upon.'

Frowning, he shook his head. 'Not spying, *senorita*, merely noticing a very attractive young blonde sitting here alone. Tea is served on the hotel terrace around the time you come here—purely a coincidence, I assure you.'

'Oh, I see. So you're a guest of the Tropic Hotel,' she surmised with a knowing nod.

'Not exactly,' he began with a shrug, 'though, as one would expect, I make myself available to the management whenever they require my services . . .'

'Ah, so you're on the staff,' she guessed, 'and that is when you've seen me. I suppose you will have a little free time until the season begins, though I believe it gets very busy here in the summer months—goodness knows how you cope.'

His lips quirked as he replied with casual modesty, 'I will endeavour to do my best.' But, although his tone remained casual, his gaze was searching as he leaned towards her to remark, 'You appeared very preoccupied when I saw you earlier. In fact, you stepped off the pavement without a glance in either direction.'

'I know, it was stupid of me,' she admitted with a reluctant sigh. 'I'd just had a disagreement with someone and my mind was not on the road.'

'Someone?' he queried, his dark brows raised.

'My sister, actually, not that it makes any difference who it was.'

'What was the trouble?' he persisted, his dark eyes compelling her attention.

'I hardly think it's any of your business!' she objected with a short laugh. 'In any case, it would be of no interest to you.'

'Why not? You may feel better if you share the problem.'

She uttered a wavering sigh. She couldn't possibly divulge the family problems which had driven Sarah here after their father, James, had discovered the new seasons' designs for his firm's fashionable sportswear were missing. He had suspected Sarah was somehow involved in their disappearance. Of course, Sarah had denied it and Garland could still recall the awful scene when her sister had stormed out of the house with the intention of coming to this holiday villa the McLeod family owned. A casual friend, Patricia Blanford, was driving to Spain and had persuaded Sarah to travel with her in what she had since described as an incredibly luxurious vehicle. Garland sighed again; much as she would welcome a sympathetic ear, it was difficult to comprehend why a total stranger—admittedly a handsome one—was questioning her quite so openly.

'So, there is something,' he decided for himself, leaning even closer as he continued to hold her gaze. 'Could it have anything to do with last night's little fiasco?'

His question came as a shock and for a moment she froze. The mere mention of last night brought the agony of humiliation flooding back; was that where she had seen him, in Don's nightclub in Barcelona? It didn't look the kind of place he would frequent yet, how else could he have known? Had he witnessed that dreadful scene when, in a voice loud enough for all to hear, Don had called her a 'Useless idiot with no ambition' plus many other unwarranted names . . .

'I don't recall seeing you there,' she managed, recovering her composure.

He shook his head and gave her a crooked smile. 'No, I was not there, but Meredith's big time around here and news travels fast. However, I would not have considered him to be your choice of escort.'

'He wasn't my escort, just a friend of my sister who offered me work. In fact, that was partly what the disagreement with Sarah was about.'

'And does this offer appeal to you?' he asked quietly.

'No, which was the cause of the trouble, he simply refused to accept it.'

'But he employs your sister, yes?'

'I don't think so, well, nothing permanent. Though she's inclined to boast about the financial benefits she's had from a couple of small driving jobs, and this is why she insists I should accept Don's offer, even temporarily.'

'I understand her friend, a Miss Blanford, is employed by him, so do I assume both ladies are drivers by profession?'

'I can't speak for Miss Blanford, I rarely see her. Actually, Sarah's an actress and wouldn't be here if it were not for the tiff she had with my father,' she confided with a burst of hollow laughter. 'I hope to persuade her to return to Edinburgh with me next week—this being the reason I'm here—but Sarah says I should not allow last night's incident to cloud my judgement, yet Meredith's the last person I would choose as my employer. For some unaccountable reason I don't trust the man, and both he and Patricia seem totally obsessed by money.'

His lips twitched with what appeared to be amusement as he remarked, 'So, you quarrel with your sister, you mistrust her friend Meredith, and you also criticise the Blanford woman. I am sure you are right but, tell me, have you good reason for this, or are you relying purely on feminine instinct?'

His expression infuriated her and she immediately regretted being so frank. Whatever she thought of Sarah, or Don, she should not have invited his opinion.

'Really, it is no concern of yours, *senor* . . . whatever your name is, and if this is to be your sole topic of conversation, then I would prefer to be left alone.'

'Please, call me Nic,' he said smoothly and, apparently unmoved by her expression of annoyance, made no effort to leave.

'Well, as you appear determined to stay, I'm leaving!' she hissed, snatching up her bag. 'I don't care to be quizzed by a total stranger.'

'Stranger?' he repeated with a deep chuckle. 'My dear Garland, I already feel I've known you for quite some time.'

Ignoring him, she left the table and walked

briskly away. And only as she was crossing the road did she realise he had called her by name. She cast a furtive glance back towards the cafe when, to her embarrassment, he raised a hand and smiled. How could he know her name, she wondered, hastening her step, how could a member of staff of the Tropic Hotel possibly know?

*   *   *

Once round the memorable bend in the road, Garland slowed her pace, still pondering the question. True, his face was vaguely familiar, but the name Nic meant nothing. Yet he clearly knew something about her otherwise why would he have mentioned last night? She was curious, but had she not left the cafe when she did she knew any further questions would have reduced her to tears.

By the time she reached the villa she had exhausted all lines of thought on Nic. And yet it suddenly occurred to her that he had shown more concern over her discomfort from the previous evening than had her own sister, or her flighty friend, Patricia. Perhaps she had over-reacted.

'Sorry, Nic—whoever you are . . .' she murmured to herself as she unlocked the door, her thoughts turning to the welcome she might receive.

Entering the house, she glanced towards the

open patio doors to see her sister stretched out on a sunbed, a mobile telephone held to her ear.

'Oh no, I'm not willing to be involved in anything illegal. I mean it, Patricia.' Garland heard her say. 'I think I can guess what you're up to . . .' Sarah's voice trailed off as she became aware of someone's reflection in the glass of the open patio door.

'Don't mind me,' said Garland, drawing back, though she wondered what it was her sister so adamantly refused to become involved with. It sounded very mysterious. Reluctant to enquire, she merely gave a casual wave and announced, 'I'm going to my room.'

'Oh don't go—come and join me,' Sarah invited, and with a brief farewell to the caller she switched off the 'phone. 'Relax a while, you look exhausted.'

'I was going to change . . .' Garland began, a trifle apprehensive over her sister's unexpected concern.

'Please,' Sarah appealed, indicating a cane chair beside her. 'I know you're unhappy, but there's no need to look so sad, not now that Don has apologised.'

Garland came to a sudden halt halfway across the patio. 'Don has apologised!' she echoed, rolling her eyes heavenwards. 'Whatever next!'

'Yes, he rang just after you left. He was so disappointed to have missed you. Actually, I

11

don't think he was feeling too well, but he didn't complain . . .'

'I should jolly-well think he didn't!' Garland cried. 'What incredible cheek!'

'Don't be hard on him, darling,' Sarah cajoled. 'You know, most girls would give anything to be in your position.'

'But I'm not most girls, Sarah, and I do wish you'd drop the subject.'

Expressing a sigh of irritation, Sarah sank back on her lounger, wriggling her trim figure into a more comfortable position. 'I think you're being very silly,' she said, 'after all, he has apologised. Anyway, he'll tell you himself later.'

Garland's head shot up. 'Later! What is that supposed to mean?'

'Patricia won't be here this evening so I have invited him to dinner which should give you an opportunity to settle any differences you may have.'

'Oh, Sarah! Can't you get it into your head, there's nothing to settle! And if he's coming here to dinner, I hope the two of you enjoy it. I'm going out!'

'Really!' Sarah gasped, but Garland turned swiftly on her heel and fled into the house with the words, 'I hope you realise you'll not get rich working for McLeods—not on the pittance Daddy pays you!' ringing in her ears.

The last remark really hurt. But she was convinced things would improve now their

12

father, James McLeod, had re-established his business. Garland hadn't forgotten his enthusiasm after he employed a new designer and business began to pick up. Once he had recovered from the shock of his wife's death the previous year, James McLeod proved he had the drive to put the manufacture and sales of his sportswear and equipment back on the market.

Sarah had then refused to be involved in getting the business back on its feet, even after her father withdrew his accusation. During a childhood illness, she had been indulged by both their parents and for as long as Garland could remember Sarah expected always to have her way. She could yet recall her sister's horror when, last autumn, she had announced her intention to give up her training as a model to work as a representative of her father's firm to reduce business expenses. And Sarah still disapproved. For the past week she had done her utmost to point out how wonderful life could be working for Don Meredith.

'Look, Sarah, if he's so wonderful, why don't you marry him?' she had snapped earlier that day when her sister had been dishing out advice.

'After Mark and I parted financial security became more important to me,' Sarah had replied bitterly, 'and that is something at which Don is extremely successful.'

Reflecting on this bitter exchange sent Garland scurrying into her bathroom. If Don was coming to dinner, she had better get moving. To suffer hearing his sickening apologies didn't bear thinking about.

*   *   *

Less than an hour later, Garland had showered and changed, and was about to leave the house with the intention of dining at Pedro's. She suspected the menu there would have little to offer in the way of cooked meals but she was willing to settle for an omelette, or a sandwich of local sweet-cured ham, rather than face Don. She shuddered, reflecting upon his embarrassing behaviour the previous evening; it was hard to believe he was the same man to whom Sarah had introduced her soon after her arrival. At first he had seemed to be quite charming, but last night, in the luxurious surroundings of his business world he had become a loud-mouthed monster.

She was startled by a knock on her bedroom door. 'Father wants a word with you,' she heard Sarah announce coolly. 'He's calling from his office.'

Picking up her bag, Garland dashed down to the sitting room. It was unusual for him to ring unless it was a matter of some urgency. Yet, when James McLeod came on the line he didn't sound the least bit anxious.

14

'Garland! You sound quite breathless,' he laughed, 'but there's nothing to worry about—in fact, it's good news.'

Had Sarah spoken to him about returning home, was the first thought that flew to mind and her hopes rose. But he then went on to give his reason for calling.

'Poor old John's had a heart attack so now there's no hope of him presenting the prizes.'

Doubting she had heard him correctly, she gasped, 'I thought you said it was good news!'

'Ach no, that's not what I meant. It's the problem of the presentation we have to consider and this is of imminent concern to us both.'

'Presentation,' Garland repeated blankly, trying to collect her thoughts. 'Presentation for what?'

'Golf, of course!' he exclaimed on a sigh of exasperation. 'It's the Pro-Am match, the day before the big tournament. Had you forgotten, we're sponsoring it this year?'

'Oh yes, of course,' she admitted uncomfortably as she recollected hearing about the event. 'But how's John? You haven't told me that.'

'He's quite stable, actually—soon be on his feet again. I've just left the hospital where we had a lengthy discussion about the problem . . .'

'So he's well enough to speak?' she broke in, puzzled that her father should telephone the news considering his partner sounded well on the way to recovery.

'Oh yes, he's quite lucid!' James McLeod exclaimed with a chuckle. 'In fact, it was his suggestion that you should take his place. And as you are less than two hours drive away from the course I was only too happy to agree,' he went on, and before she had the chance to object continued, 'You are ideal for the job, Garland—young, attractive—daughter of the company boss—absolutely ideal!'

'Oh no! Couldn't you have asked Sarah?'

'Darling, I already have and, as I anticipated, she refused so now I'm asking you—no, begging you.'

Garland's brain was in a whirl. 'You want me to present the prizes! You're joking, Pops . . .'

'No, darling, I'm serious—so serious I have cancelled your flight. And I've faxed the organisers to let them know of the change of plan, though it shouldn't make any difference to them—unless they want to order a bouquet for you,' he ended on a jovial note.

'But I don't know the first thing about golf!' she cried desperately.

'I'm asking you to present the prizes, not play!' he pointed out, adding shrewdly, 'And, don't forget, as a representative of this company, it's your duty. It will be valuable experience for you, an opportunity to do business. Believe me, Garland, our new

16

designs are really something!'

'But you know I don't deal in men's sportswear . . .' she started to object, then felt herself weakening. 'Oh well, if it means so much to you, Pops . . .' she said, a faint note of defeat creeping into her voice, 'maybe I could stay on a little longer.'

'Because of Don, I assume?' he suggested, though without enthusiasm.

She laughed. 'No, that's not the reason.' She lowered her voice in case Sarah was within earshot, to add, 'He's out of the picture completely.'

'Thank goodness for that!' he exclaimed. 'I met the man only briefly when I was over there and took an instant dislike to him.'

'You've spoken to Sarah?' she queried in the same lowered tone.

'Just a few words,' he replied on a sighing breath. 'Is she well?'

'Fine,' she assured him and whispered, 'though it's my guess she'll eventually become bored with this place, you know what she's like.'

'I pray you're right,' he responded in a choked voice when her own anxiety over extending her stay faded. It meant more time to work on Sarah.

James McLeod cleared his throat. 'Let's get back to business,' he continued. 'I've arranged for one of our young reps to join you. He's well acquainted with the golf scene and he can

17

attend to any orders that come our way. Also, I've booked a hotel room for you in the city, which will mean less travelling, and you'll be able to attend the celebration dinners. You'll need to look your best at the presentation so buy yourself a couple of dresses. Got a pen and paper handy?' he asked and went on the reel off the young representative's name, the name of the hotel, and numerous other items as they came to mind.

Garland was in a whirl by the time she had replaced the receiver. To be staying longer than she had originally expected was a daunting prospect. But, annoyed though she had been at the time, Nic had been in her thoughts since that afternoon and there now was a possibility they might meet up at Pedro's again. However, presenting the prizes was an entirely different matter and could prove to be a nerve-racking experience, but a challenge she had to meet for the sake of the firm.

*   *   *

Garland had anticipated another confrontation with Sarah before she left, and had barely returned the receiver to its rest when her sister appeared in the room.

'Where are you going?' she demanded, her eyes travelling over the silky blue dress Garland was wearing.

Garland responded with an evasive smile as

18

she flicked back her newly washed curls. 'I haven't yet decided so don't wait up, I have a key.'

'But what about Don—where shall I suggest he meets you?' she asked tightly in an effort to stifle her annoyance.

'Tell him anything you like,' said Garland as Sarah followed her out of the room, and shooting her a wide smile added, 'With luck I won't be there.'

'Really!' Sarah snorted. 'You're just like father—so impetuous . . .'

Leaving her fuming in the hallway, Garland set off down the slope towards the little town. In the growing darkness she could pick out the lights of the fishing boats as they left the tiny harbour, and caught the occasional beam of headlights moving along the promenade. She drew a deep breath, enjoying the balmy, perfumed evening air in the silence of the country road. She could well understand her sister's preference for this climate; so very different from the chilly outskirts of Edinburgh in spring. Yet, picturing her father at home relaxing before a huge log fire made her feel suddenly sad. It really hurt to find Sarah preferred the villa to being curled up by the fire in the easy company of her father in the family home. She uttered a wavering sigh, reflecting on the heartbreak he'd felt over Sarah's leaving almost three months ago. As a result, this holiday had been decided upon with the hope she could induce her sister to return home. But it had all gone wrong, Sarah wouldn't even discuss it, her sole interest being to live a life of luxury in the company of her wealthy but vulgar friends.

She had reached the corner now and clicked her tongue in self-reproach, remembering the moment when she had inadvertently stepped in front of Nic's car. But this time she continued along the pavement until she was opposite the cafe, ensuring the road was clear before she crossed.

Taking a seat at her usual table on the patio, she glanced at her watch. It was rather early for dining so she decided to take an aperitif to pass the time, and Pedro's brows rose in surprise when she ordered a very dry sherry instead of the usual tea. Hurriedly tying on his apron, he went off to prepare her order, obviously delighted by her unexpected appearance.

The parasols had been folded away for the evening and Garland sipped her drink and nibbled an olive in the subdued light of the lamp suspended from the cafe wall. Thoughtfully twirling the glass in her fingers, she was enveloped by a feeling of desolation as she stared on to the empty road. Yet, lonely as she was, she felt far more comfortable here than she knew she would be at the villa, making conversation with Don and Sarah, listening to his insincere apology and her sister's inveigling chatter. Her gaze strayed to the Tropic Hotel opposite where she noticed a glow from a few of the curtained windows, otherwise the place looked deserted. She felt still a trifle guilty over the way she had dismissed the stranger that afternoon, and only now did she realise she hadn't paid for her afternoon tea. Should she offer Pedro the money, or had the stranger already paid?

A couple of local men went inside to take a dark coffee, leaning on the bar as they spoke to Pedro and casting her the occasional interested glance through the open window. She was beginning to feel rather conspicuous sitting there alone yet, glancing again at her watch, saw it was still quite early for dining. She sighed, her eyes travelling back to the brightly lit bar when Pedro's quick smile brought a sudden lump to her throat. To cover her confusion she quickly swallowed the remainder of her drink and rose from the table.

Deciding to ask Pedro about the bill for the tea later, she left payment for the drink beside the empty glass. This was no time to wallow in the misery of her family troubles; she had brought her association with Don Meredith to an end, surely that was something to celebrate. But how was she to disport herself, alone, without someone to share the joy of her new-found freedom. She had an urge to do something really outrageous, something of which Sarah would strongly disapprove, anything that would erase the tension and sadness from her thoughts. But, she realised as she strolled on towards the wide moonlit beach, until Sarah agreed to return home that sadness would remain.

The soft sand was cool under her bare feet as she wandered along by the water's edge, her sandals swinging from her hand. She had succeeded in shaking off the depression which had threatened to overwhelm her, and now luxuriated in the tranquillity of her surroundings. Determined to blank the misery completely from her mind, she rushed into the sea, splashing through the gentle waves with childish glee that turned to stifled squeals of laughter as the chill of the water penetrated her flesh.

Standing knee-deep in the sea she gazed up at the rising moon, its pathway of twinkling reflections stretching to the horizon. What would Sarah and Don think if they could see her now she wondered rebelliously, and gathering up the hem of her dress she turned to dash through the water, heading back towards the beach, a glittering spray rising in her wake.

Now the sand felt warm to her feet, and she uttered a breathless cry of exhilaration as she drew to a sudden halt, fascinated by the patterns of light filtering through the palm trees lining the promenade. But as her gaze travelled along the line of twinkling lights her heart gave a jolt when a dark figure appeared, silhouetted against them, standing barely six feet away.

CHAPTER TWO

As the tall, shadowy figure advanced towards her she saw it was the man she had met at the café in the afternoon and her heart resumed its normal pace.

'You almost scared me out of my wits!' she gasped. 'How long have you been watching me?'

'Long enough to satisfy myself you were not contemplating suicide,' came his mocking reply. 'But, had I considered it to be a possibility, I most certainly would have intervened.'

'Nothing quite so dramatic,' she assured him, tugging at the sodden hem of her dress where it clung uncomfortably to her legs. 'I just felt like doing something reckless, but I expect it must have appeared pretty stupid to you.'

'If you enjoyed it, then it is not stupid, though I imagine it was a little colder than you anticipated.'

'It was rather, and I'm grateful for your concern,' she agreed politely yet, after the way she had spoken to him that afternoon, felt she didn't deserve such thoughtfulness on his part. She gave a wry smile. 'Earlier today I almost threw myself under your car, and now I appear to be about to drown myself—who could blame you for thinking me quite mad.'

'Mad no, but if I recall correctly you were a trifle piqued when you left the cafe this afternoon.' He laughed softly, his dark eyes glittering in the light of the moon as he surveyed her breathless state. 'I am inclined to suspect you are an impetuous young lady, yes?'

'You sound just like my bossy sister,' she chided laughingly, almost losing her balance as she tried to brush the sand from her feet.

'Heaven forbid!' he exclaimed under his breath. Extending a supporting hand he offered, 'Why not come to my room to dry off?'

'I'm not that impetuous!' she retaliated, stooping to retrieve her sandals. 'Don't worry, it's thin material—a brisk walk along the prom—it will soon dry.'

'Then, I will join you,' he said, retaining his hold as he escorted her over the beach to a seat where he proceeded to brush the sand from her feet.

At first she found the situation amusing—if only Sarah could see her now—and picturing her sister's horrified expression she couldn't suppress her laughter. But her laughter died suddenly and she quickly drew her foot away;

there was something quite sensuous about the way he ran his long fingers over her instep, almost a caress and strangely disturbing.

After she had slipped on her sandals he helped her to her feet to enquire, 'Are you returning home for dinner, or would you consider dining out somewhere?'

'Actually, I'd planned to eat at Pedro's, though I don't suppose there will be a great deal of choice on the menu.'

'Rather than the Tropic?' he queried with some surprise.

She cast him a smiling sideways glance. 'You're bound to recommend it.'

'Naturally,' he agreed, 'it is the only hotel open at present.'

'Do you usually take your meals in the hotel?'

'Some,' he replied with a shrug, 'though I try to keep to a healthy diet.'

'I expect you get sick of the sight of food, especially if you're involved in the preparation or the serving.'

'No, I'd be hopeless in the kitchen,' he chuckled. 'Do you enjoy cooking?'

Was he angling for an invitation? Garland wondered and smiled. 'Yes, but my sister won't allow me in the kitchen. I don't think she trusts me.'

He paused and turned to look at her. 'So, your sister does the cooking, yes?'

There was a hint of derision in Garland's

laughter. 'No fear! She's not the least bit domesticated. A local woman comes in to cook, and she employs another to do the cleaning.'

'A lady of leisure?' he suggested with a lift of one dark brow.

'Huh, she likes to think so!' Garland shot back. Then, ashamed of her outburst, she shrugged and continued evenly, 'My sister enjoys the life here.'

He nodded. 'And you, Garland?' he queried, coming to a halt beneath the feathery shadow of a tall palm. 'Do you also prefer this way of life?'

For a moment his question confused her. Unable to give an immediate response, she substituted lightly, 'Before we go any further, there's something I've been meaning to ask. How is it that you know my name?'

He gave a slight lift of his shoulders. 'This is a small town, you are a stranger here,' he explained, adding smoothly, 'and a very attractive one, too.'

She smiled at his easy compliment—a little flattery was doing her good—but she was quite unprepared for his next question, and the casual manner in which he put it to her.

'And what of your gentleman friend—your sister's employer, I believe—how does he figure in your plans for the future?' he queried in a manner so offhand she wondered if she had misheard.

26

She was checking the hem of her dress when he spoke, smoothing out the fabric, by now almost dry. At first she felt a rush of indignation, but when she raised her head and saw his expression of quiet concern it quickly subsided.

'Oh, well . . . the er, gentleman you refer to doesn't figure in my plans at all,' she told him, albeit a trifle reluctantly. 'As a matter of fact, right now he's having dinner with my sister which is why I'm here.'

He shot her a faintly puzzled frown. 'It is your wish to avoid him?'

'It most certainly is!' she replied emphatically. 'He's the last person I want to see, this evening or any other.'

'Perhaps you will regret turning away from Meredith,' he suggested with a lift of one dark brow. 'Wealth and position are assets many girls desire.'

'You may consider his position an asset, but I don't!' she shot back.

'So, last night's incident was more serious than I first thought,' he concluded gently. 'Were you very distressed?'

'No, not really,' she denied with a lift of her chin. But however firm her denial, she could do nothing to control the quiver of her lip, or blink away the sparkle of sudden tears.

'I'm sorry,' he murmured. 'This has upset you more than I realised.'

They had come to a halt beneath one of the

27

ornamental lamps illuminating the promenade when she quickly averted her face to conceal her distress. But, too late, he caught the glitter of an escaping tear and reached for her hand to give it a comforting squeeze.

Furious with herself for allowing her emotions to show, she looked up. 'Thanks, Nic. Quite frankly, I hope I never come in contact with him again.'

Nic smiled, his eyes travelling over her appraisingly as he said in a gentle voice, 'I'm sure you will have no difficulty replacing him. Now, if that dress is dry, let's have a drink before we dine.'

She gave a shaky little laugh. 'Thanks, I'd like that.'

They strolled back along the promenade in total silence. Not that it was disagreeable, Nic was relaxing company and, after her short burst of emotion, she experienced a welcome feeling of tranquillity as she gazed up to the starlit sky and listened to the gentle rippling of the waves on the darkened beach. Absorbed in the peaceful surroundings she wasn't aware of the open limousine driving slowly along the road towards them. And she was totally shocked when Nic drew her roughly against him, imprisoning her between his lean body and the hard trunk of a palm.

'It's Meredith!' he hissed, muffling her anticipated cry of protest against his chest as the car drew near. But when she struggled and pulled her head aside to utter a choking cry, his mouth came down to silence her as he continued to hold her prisoner in his arms.

Only when the purr of the powerful engine had faded into the distance did he raise his head, retaining his hold on her trembling body.

For a moment, Garland could only stare up at him in confusion, her bruised lips slightly apart. She had been rigid against him during this onslaught, but now felt her legs would buckle beneath her should he release his hold.

'That was Meredith's car,' he said, his eyes still on the road. 'Could he have been searching for you?'

Finding her voice, she thrust him away to say unevenly, 'Yes, I expect he was. Even so, there was no need for that!'

'After what you said earlier, I assumed you would not wish to be seen,' he growled, his breathing a trifle harsh. And his dark eyes narrowed as he continued, 'Or have I got the wrong impression?'

She shook her head vigorously. 'Oh no, I'm glad he didn't see me. But how did you know it was his car?'

'I see it often, usually driven at high speed, but judging by the unusually slow pace he was driving this evening it was obvious he was looking for someone.'

She let out a ragged breath. 'Thanks for preventing him spotting me, though I do wish you'd warned me,' she complained, fingering her slightly swollen lip.

'If I hadn't acted quickly he would have heard you,' he said on a sigh of exasperation. 'In the circumstances, what other method would you suggest?'

'You could have told me to keep still!' she rebuked him unreasonably. Yet, even though she knew she was being unreasonable, had he not shielded her from view, without doubt it would have resulted in a scene. But there was something curiously disturbing about being overpowered by Nic. During those few unexpected moments she had been conscious of his strength and the warm, spicy scent of his cologne which lingered still in her nostrils.

Regarding her petulant expression with amusement, he said, 'I suppose I could, but I preferred my method.'

Relieved to have escaped Don's notice she relaxed and suggested, 'Most likely he'll look for me in the hotel so let's go to Pedro's. Anyway, I owe you a drink. It didn't occur to me until I'd left that I hadn't paid for my afternoon tea, and I'd much prefer one of Pedro's more secluded tables, if you have no objection.'

'Objection!' he echoed laughingly, 'I'd be delighted!' And as they neared the cafe he continued, 'I must confess, I had hoped to see you again.'

Her spirits rose. 'As it happens, I shall not be leaving here for a few more days yet . . .'

'Ah no—that is unfortunate—I shall be away for the remainder of the week.' he told her with a rueful smile as he led her to a candlelit table, sheltered from view by a vine-covered trellis.

'Oh well, it doesn't matter,' she put in quickly, taking the seat Nic held for her, when she wondered if it had been a mistake to invite him to join her here. He may get the impression she was already seeking a replacement for Don and consider her friendliness a welcome to any advance he cared to make. There again, was she using Nic simply to spite her sister? Sarah would be completely aghast to learn she had dined with a member of staff from the Tropic Hotel. She shivered with pleasure just thinking about it.

Pedro came out to discuss the dishes available that evening. 'It's a sizeable menu,' she remarked, beginning to feel quite hungry. Even the unexpected incident along the promenade hadn't served to dull her appetite and, considering the variety on offer, she was pleased to note the prices were low. The hotel may not pay him a very high wage and tips would be few just now. Even so, he appeared remarkably well groomed, she noticed, and his clothes looked to be of good quality. Did he spend his entire earnings preserving his immaculate appearance? Was he perhaps a ladies man? The thought was a trifle unsettling.

'Pedro assures me the local dishes are excellent—that is, providing you are adventurous,' Nic said as the proprietor waited to take their order. But as Pedro's English was reserved for the more simple phrases, Nic reverted to his familiar tongue then translated to her with ease. His English was almost perfect—only a hint of an accent which she found quite attractive.

'Your English is good,' she remarked. 'It must be an advantage when the hotel is patronised by the British. Where did you learn to speak so well?'

'During my time at college, and then England,' he told her and returned his attention to the menu.

'What subject were you studying? Was it connected with the work you are doing now, or do you intend to visit England again?'

'No, not really, I simply enjoy languages.' he said with a dismissive movement of his hand. 'I have no immediate plans to travel.'

Her smile faded and her cheeks grew pink. 'Sorry, I didn't mean to pry,' she murmured, a trifle piqued.

'Ah, forgive me, I did not intend to offend you, but I don't wish to bore you with my problems . . .'

'Problems?' she queried, glancing at his hands. 'Are you married?'

'No no, I have no such ties, I assure you,' he said with another dismissive gesture. Then, flashing her a smile, he said softly, 'Let us forget our troubles and enjoy the evening together, yes?'

'That suits me,' she responded a little stiffly, but she couldn't help wondering what it was that prevented him from disclosing a few unimportant facts about his life, particularly since he'd delved far deeper into hers. There again, it was still possible he had a wife tucked away somewhere, even though he wore no plain gold band on his finger.

'Now, let us decide what we shall eat,' he said, and after some discussion on certain dishes, they settled for Xato, a regional salad with anchovies and a hot, spicy sauce, and local sausage served with white beans to follow.

'You must feel a little chilled after being in the water,' Nic commented when Pedro withdrew from setting out the cutlery and pouring the wine.

'No no, I'm fine,' she assured him taking a sip of her wine, its coolness soothing her bruised lip. Actually, her feet were tingling now, and his unwavering regard had brought a rush of warm colour to her cheeks, quite beyond her control.

'Good,' he murmured, his dark eyes glittering in the candlelight before he glanced past her to say, 'Ah, here comes Pedro with our Xato.'

She smiled as Pedro set down the dish with

an even greater flourish than when he had laid out the cutlery. And when his daughter followed to place a flower-filled vase beside it her blue eyes widened. 'We're being treated like celebrities!' she exclaimed, admiring the beautifully garnished dish. 'It looks simply delicious, I must come here more often,'

Nic glanced up from beneath his thick, dark lashes. 'I hope you do,' he said softly, 'also that I will have another opportunity to join you during your stay.'

'I would have thought you'd be busy in the hotel most evenings,' she said, and aware of his frequent glances in its direction, commented, 'though I expect it is fairly quiet just now.'

He looked at her for a moment, a flicker of a smile playing on his lips as he said, 'I am sure they will manage without me. More wine?'

As the next course arrived, Garland sipped thoughtfully of her wine, puzzling over Nic's reluctance to reveal anything about himself. She found it to be slightly hurtful, otherwise she was enjoying being with him; a contrast to her recent outings in the company of Sarah's social circle. Here there was none of the meaningless chatter to endure, or artificial smiles to acknowledge, and no Sarah or Patricia to draw her attention to some well-known face in the crowd. It was so tranquil sitting in this secluded corner with only the faint sound of laughter drifting from the bar. But she knew this peace couldn't last; it was but a temporary respite from her unhappy experiences over the past few days.

She glanced up to find Nic's gaze upon her, his dark brows raised enquiringly. 'Sorry, I was miles away,' she confessed. 'Were you speaking?'

'I merely asked if you had enjoyed your meal,' he said. 'Personally, I was pleasantly surprised.'

She sighed contentedly and sank back in her chair. 'Delicious,' she said. 'Quite frankly, I haven't felt so relaxed in ages.'

He smiled, leaning forward to rest his elbows on the table to ask, 'And when we have finished coffee, what would you like to do?'

Garland gave a tiny giggle. 'You shouldn't allow me such freedom of choice, I may want to paddle again.'

Nic chuckled. 'I don't think so, but why not tomorrow when it is warmer?'

'That's fine by me,' she agreed, setting down her cup. 'Shall we meet on the beach around eleven.'

He nodded, his expression more serious as he started to say, 'Yes, I would like that but, before we go any further, there is something I should explain . . .'

'Oh don't get all serious and spoil everything,' she laughed. 'I have really enjoyed myself this evening, for the first time since I arrived.'

'I expect it will keep,' he said with a shrug,

and reaching for his wallet he rose from the table.

'Hey—it's my turn . . .' she began, opening her bag. 'I left you with the bill for tea, remember?'

His long fingers closed over hers. 'My pleasure,' he said firmly, raising a hand to catch Pedro's attention through the window. Seeing her expression of dismay he added with a grin, 'Don't worry, Garland, the hotel pays me a reasonable wage.'

Murmuring her thanks as he went off in search of Pedro, she took out her compact to glance in the mirror. Her lip was only slightly swollen, she noted thankfully; nothing Sarah's sharp eyes would detect.

She became aware Nic had seen her studying her reflection as he approached. Cupping her chin in his warm fingers, he raised her face to the light.

'Sorry about that,' he said with a rueful smile, and she held her breath as he scanned her face before lowering his head to murmur, 'I can also be very gentle.' And his lips sought hers in the way he promised, brushing them lightly, tantalisingly, until hers parted in sensual response.

His kiss left her slightly breathless but not wishing he should be aware of the effect he had upon her, Garland lowered her eyes.

'Yes, a very impetuous young lady,' he breathed softly, holding her at arms length.

'Perhaps a little,' she confessed in a wavering voice. That was the second time he'd made such a comment. But was he referring to the way she had dashed into the water, or was it the manner in which she had responded to his kiss? Now she had the opportunity to prolong her visit she was more hopeful of continuing her friendship with Nic.

Just then, the melodic tones of a mobile telephone sounded from the pocket of Nic's jacket. In moments he had it held to his ear, and his expression grew tense as he listened to the caller's voice, making only the briefest of responses himself. 'Forgive me,' he said as he returned the mobile to his pocket, 'I must get back to the hotel. Do you have a car?'

'No need, I like to walk.'

'I will order a taxi for you,' he insisted, then went on to enquire, 'Incidentally, does your sister own a car?'

Thinking it a rather strange question, she frowned. 'Not at present . . .'

'You are sure?'

'Quite sure. Now please, I realise you are needed so it is not necessary for you to wait until the taxi arrives.' She gave him a mischievous smile as she added, 'You'd better get back to work—maybe some old colonel is waiting for his nightcap.'

He walked away, his soft chuckle drifting back to her as he crossed the road.

*　　　*　　　*

'Where were you last night?' Sarah asked as she and Garland sat down to breakfast. 'Don looked everywhere and he sounded most upset when he telephoned me from the hotel.'

Garland shrugged. 'Here and there,' she replied evasively, reaching for the coffee jug.

'He was sure you would be dining at the Tropic.'

'Actually, I ate a very satisfying meal at Pedro's . . .'

'You're not going to give a very good impression dining in a place like that,' Sarah broke in. 'What would my friends have thought if they'd seen you.'

'If they had seen me, they will tell you I wasn't alone,' Garland informed her with a devilish grin. 'In fact, I was accompanied by one of the staff from the hotel.'

'One of the staff!' cried Sarah incredulously. 'Are you saying you allowed yourself to be picked up by someone like that?'

'Oh, Sarah, you're such a snob,' Garland derided smilingly. 'I found him to be most charming—and sober,' she stressed with a hint of triumph.

Sarah cast her younger sister a furious glance and crashed the coffee pot down on the table. 'Well, you succeeded in teaching Don a lesson—presuming that was your intention—so perhaps now we can revert to normal living.'

'I don't wish to revert to anything with Don,' Garland told her, striving to suppress her exasperation. 'Can't you understand, Sarah—he's not the man I thought him to be when we first were introduced—I dislike him intensely.'

'I think you are behaving quite stupidly,' Sarah returned, her unyielding manner trying Garland's patience. 'In fact, you're making it rather difficult for me.'

'Stupid or not, last night I felt more relaxed than I ever did in Don's company,' Garland shot back. And with Nic's parting kiss still clearly imprinted in her thoughts, she gave Sarah an apologetic smile.

Sarah's tone changed. 'But, darling, Don has promised it won't happen again,' she wheedled.' It would be only fair to give him another chance.'

Garland uttered a deep sigh and pointed out, 'I have now been here for more than a week and during the last two days Don has behaved insufferably. I couldn't possibly agree to being employed by a man like that!'

Sarah cut through her slice of toast with more than necessary vigour. 'So, you would prefer to associate with a mere waiter, or whatever he is, who hasn't a penny to his name!' she spat out. 'Tell me, just what kind of future has he to offer?'

'I've only just met the man!' Garland exclaimed incredulously. 'In any case, I'm not interested in what he has to offer, it's his personality which counts!'

Sarah cast her a withering glance. 'Personality!' she hissed scornfully. 'I doubt anyone in his position possesses a very stimulating personality.'

'Well it most certainly is not as mercenary as yours!' Garland retorted.

'Ah, but can you be certain this er, friend of yours is not merely hankering after you because he thinks you have money?'

Garland smiled. 'Are you suggesting he's using your tactics? Both you and Patricia seem always to be around if someone's flashing their cash about.'

Sarah pursed her ruby lips. 'I suppose my father filled your head with those ideas after he accused me of selling his stupid designs.'

'He didn't accuse you, he merely asked why your friend Patricia had shown such an interest in them.'

Sarah's eyes narrowed. 'Maybe, but nothing was proved against either of us so I suggest you watch your tongue!'

'Then can you explain where your money comes from? It's almost six months since you did any acting, either in films or on stage, and they were only bit parts.'

'Now look here, I'm not standing for this! Who did you think looked after Mummy while you were at modeling school?'

'It most certainly wasn't you, Sarah. Once I was back home you broke off your engagement and went gallivanting round Europe. Your beastly friend, Don happened to let that slip the other night!'

Ignoring her sister's venomous glance, Garland rose from the table. 'By the way, Sarah, do you own a car?'

'A car?' she repeated, looking quite startled. 'No, I don't. Why do you ask—who wants to know?'

'Calm down, I'm just curious. But now it's time I got ready for when the taxi arrives,' she said. 'There's been a change of plan, I'm meeting Simon, one of Daddy's reps in the city this morning.'

Sarah appeared almost overcome with relief. Letting out a long breath, she said, 'Ah, now I understand. Were you hoping I could give you a lift?'

*   *   *

Nic wasn't around when Garland called at the Tropic the following morning. The girl at reception looked surprised when she asked for him but agreed to pass on her note explaining her appointment in the city, which meant she would not be able to meet him as arranged. But Nic continued to remain in her thoughts throughout the journey until the bustling city streets echoing with the sound of blaring horns captured her attention. Eventually, the taxi pulled up before a hotel situated in a wide, tree-lined avenue with buildings towering on either side, and she saw Simon waiting in the doorway.

'Good to see you!' said Simon, shooting her a friendly grin as he tipped the driver. And as he ushered her across the cool marble-floored reception area he told her, 'Your father suggested I come a day earlier so that we have the opportunity to spend more time together. I've ordered coffee to be served in the lounge as I felt sure you'd like to settle in before we make a start.'

'That was thoughtful of you, Simon. I must admit I'm quite nervous about the whole thing as I know absolutely nothing about golf.'

'You don't need to, your role is to look pretty . . . and smile,' he added, noting her serious expression as they entered the lounge. 'I'm sure you can manage to appear interested in the game, if only for the sake of the firm.'

'I don't seem to have much choice,' she laughed, taking a seat on the sprawling leather settee. 'Also, I've had instructions to do a little shopping for the event so perhaps you'll point me in the right direction.'

'We'll go before lunch,' he decided, sliding the tray of coffee to one side of the low table to make room for his briefcase, 'but first, I'll give you a brief outline of what is happening tomorrow. Then, if there are any points you wish me to clarify, we shall have plenty of time.'

While Garland poured coffee, Simon proceeded to spread a map of the course in front of her, indicating the vantage points with a good view of play, and the clubhouse with its specially erected stand where the presentation would be made. Next he drew out a programme which listed the names of players, many well-known characters of stage, television, and radio and explained they would be teamed with the professional golfers. Simon's eyes rolled ceiling-wards at Garland's gasp of pleasure when she noted one of her favourite pop singers listed along with his photograph.

'At least you'll be in a position to get his autograph,' Simon teased. 'In fact, you will meet many famous names so it won't be quite as boring as you expected,' he added, drawing yet another brochure from his briefcase. 'For myself, this event is terrific, and with luck I should get a game with one or two of these chaps. They're top names,' he emphasised, his young face aglow as he spread open the illustrated brochure to name the professional players one by one.

Simon's enthusiasm was a little infectious and Garland felt her spirits rise. She did recall some of the names and more familiar faces from the television when her father watched play at home. But she'd never shown more than scant interest, until now, when it had become a duty for the sake of the firm.

Listening to her colleague, it seemed he knew a great deal about the background of each player 'This chap is from Portugal,' he told her. 'And I've seen this fellow play in Scotland, and he's Italian.' Simon knew them all. And running his forefinger down the list he continued, 'These are local fellows, though this chap is a professional who has been out of the game for some time—an accident, I believe—so it will be interesting to see what sort of come-back he makes.'

Simon's finger had come to rest beneath a photograph of a dark-haired man, causing Garland to draw a sharp breath. There, staring up from the page was a familiar image— questioning dark eyes above a firm mouth and chin—and, beneath it, in bold letters, the name NICOLAU MARAGALL!

CHAPTER THREE

'He is the player I was telling you about,' Simon was saying, completely oblivious to Garland's shocked expression. 'Before his accident he won almost every tournament— became quite a wealthy man—so it's great to see him back in the game.'

Speechless, Garland stared at the photograph of the man who had lingered in her thoughts since they'd had dinner together the previous evening. And it took a gentle nudge from Simon to bring her back to the present.

'Hey, you look as though you've seen a ghost!' he exclaimed laughingly then, realising she found the remark anything but humorous, continued with more concern, 'Do I take it you already know him?'

Garland closed her eyes for a moment before she managed a shaky reply. 'Y-yes, we have met—only briefly—b-but at the time I didn't know he was the player you were speaking of.'

'I see. So is there a chance of you introducing me? Maybe you can persuade him to give me a game.'

'I thought we were here to work!' she said sharply but, the very moment she had spoken, realised she had no right to vent her pent up emotions on Simon and one glance at his hurt expression brought an immediate apology to her lips. 'I'm sorry, Simon, I shouldn't have said that, I'm just a bit on edge.'

Simon shot her a rueful smile. 'I hadn't realised it was a touchy subject. Want to talk about it?'

'Not really,' she murmured, dropping her eyes. 'You see, he allowed me to think he was a member of staff at the Tropic Hotel, though why he chose to conceal his true identity I can't imagine. Quite frankly, Simon, I don't want to see him ever again.'

Simon's expression grew more serious before he revealed, 'That could prove to be rather difficult, he's sure to be amongst the winners. But don't let it worry you, with your looks you'll be the centre of attention.'

'That's just it, I don't want his attention!' she cried, convinced she couldn't bear to face Nic now his deception had come to light. 'Oh please, Simon,' she pleaded, 'can't you find someone else? The very thought of all those people terrifies me, I don't think I can face it . . .'

'You don't think you can face it!' he expostulated. 'Just where do you think I can find someone to take your place at such short notice? Really, Garland, you surprise me, I thought I could depend on you!'

'Well you can't,' she returned petulantly, 'I'm sorry, but that's how it is.'

'I see,' he said in a more controlled voice. 'When things get tough, you withdraw your support, just like your sister.'

That really shook Garland. 'I'm not in the least like my sister!' she cried, her colour rising. 'I've always stood by the firm, and you know it . . .'

'Then stand by it now,' he demanded, though not unkindly. 'If you don't, I'm going to look a complete idiot and McLeod's reputation will suffer badly.'

Garland let out a ragged sigh. She felt trapped, but what could she say to explain her predicament? He would consider her rather silly if he knew she had lost her heart to Nic Maragall in so short a time. He wouldn't understand. But she didn't want to appear unwilling to give the business her full support.'

'Well?' Simon queried on a hopeful note. 'Do I take your silence to mean you have reconsidered?'

It was a few moments before Garland could bring herself to reply though she knew the answer her colleague expected. 'I don't want you to think I'd let you down without good reason,' she began hesitantly. 'It's just . . .'

'That's the spirit!' he interjected. 'I knew you could do it.'

A wave of dismay washed over her; yet she couldn't possibly divulge her feelings for Nic, particularly now when she had discovered him to be someone who Simon greatly admired.

'Oh, Simon, you're an absolute bully!' she exclaimed. 'You've no idea how awkward this is going to be.'

Simon shot her a look of obvious relief. 'You ought to know me by now—I don't give in easily.'

'That's the trouble, both you and my father know me well enough to be confident I won't let you down,' she responded testily.

Simon smiled. 'I'm pleased you changed your mind. There's no-one I'd rather be with on this job than you, Garland.'

'The feeling's mutual, and I hope you didn't

think I was trying to back out because of you.'

He laughed. 'No, but it's my guess some other guy is to blame for your reluctance to take part. It can't be this Meredith fellow, your father told me that's off, so I'm certain Nic Maragall has something to do with it.'

Ignoring that remark, she returned her attention to the brochures so that Simon should not see the effect his speculation had upon her. But again her eyes met Nic's image staring up from the glossy page, his smiling face playing havoc with her emotions.

Tearing her gaze from the picture she looked up to ask with forced brightness, 'Well, what happens next? I'm relying on you to tell me what's expected of me.'

Simon looked relieved and gathered up the brochures. 'I think we can leave these for the moment,' he said. 'I'll make sure you have a list of the order of play before the game starts, and you have a full day in which to relax tomorrow and rehearse your speech. After lunch I want to visit the course and check on the display stands in case the sales team have left anything out. We have a new line in shirts with the firm's emblem picked out in gold on the breast pocket,' he told her with enthusiasm. 'I want them displayed in a prominent position.'

'We have the same emblem on ladies swimwear and it looks terrific!' she approved, striving to equal his keenness. 'I expect this is a busy time for you, Simon, particularly when you have a raw recruit like me tagging along.'

'I had most of the planning organised before I came,' he told her confidently. 'Don't forget, this is my second year here, and the sales team are experienced so I don't think we need worry.'

Surprised by his confidence, considering he was only twenty-four—only slightly older than herself—she asked, 'Doesn't my part in this worry you?'

'Not really, I've prepared a rough guide to your speech. We can run through it before you leave, then if there's anything you want to add let me know when you return tomorrow evening. But first, let's finish our coffee before I point you in the direction of the shops where you can buy the dresses you want.'

*   *   *

Garland felt quite exhausted by the time she dropped her purchases on the bed in Simon's hotel room. He had directed her to a number of fashionable shops nearby where she had bought two dresses, a matching bag, and high-heeled sandals. But even that short walk in the heat of the mid-day sun had tired her and, together with the constant puzzle over Nic, she seemed drained of energy. Why couldn't he have been frank with her? Did he have a notorious reputation to conceal, or was there a more sinister side to his character he wished to hide? It must be something he felt unable to confide and, although it was not her concern, she felt slighted yet, at the same time, intrigued.

A tap on the door brought her back to the present and she began to remove the dresses from their packing, intending to leave them here in Simon's wardrobe.

'By the size of those bags you appear to have bought everything you need,' he remarked as she beckoned him in. 'Now, I suggest we have lunch early as I don't want to be too late going to the course.'

'Good of you to let me leave them here,' she said, sliding the dresses onto hangers, 'but I'm not terribly hungry so I'll just come and watch you eat.'

'Frightened you'll not be able to get into those outfits,' he grinned, his gaze raking over her slim figure admiringly. 'I must say, I approve your choice.'

*   *   *

Down in the dining room, Garland toyed with a mixed salad, her thoughts still dwelling on Nic when she wondered if he had continued with his plan to go to the beach. Unaware of the hurt she was suffering, Simon kept up a cheerful account of what had taken place at the last tournament he had managed for her father.

'Once the winners have been announced, the prize-giving takes place,' he said, coming back to the present tournament. 'And, don't worry, I'll give you your cue when it's time for the presentation. 'The President will introduce you, probably in English, then you step forward to deliver your few words of congratulation to the winners.'

'That's the part I most dread,' she reminded him, omitting to add that her greater fear was with what followed, should Nic be in line for a prize.

'It's only a short speech and I'll be there to remind you of the names of winners,' he assured her. 'All you have to do is hand over the prizes. Nothing to it!'

'Wish I had your confidence,' she groaned. 'Perhaps I ought to take notes during the game to enable me to make one or two sensible comments afterwards.'

'You've got the idea,' he grinned. 'And should Maragall be amongst the winners you could say how pleased you are to see him back on the course.'

'Was his a very bad accident?' she asked, feigning casual interest.

'Got hit by a car. I gather there was something suspicious about it, or so I read in the paper,' Simon related, 'and I believe Nic refused to speak to the press so I'm not sure exactly what happened. Now, eat up or we

51

shall be late. I can fill you in with details of the tournament on the way to the course.'

*   *   *

Garland was filled with admiration for the way Simon handled the hired car through the traffic in the busy city, travelling in a southward direction to reach the course where the tournament was to take place. She was glad of the slight breeze coming in through the open roof as they drove along, through the outskirts of the city with its backdrop of high mountains cloaked in a sunny haze. For one crazy moment she wished it could be Nic in the driving seat. But no, better he's not she reminded herself. Like Don Meredith, he was not a man to be trusted.

'Nearly there,' Simon announced as they turned off the main road into a well kept drive edged with grass and shrubs in glorious shades of green. Ahead, a large building came into view, and beyond it rows of stands with awnings in vivid colours to provide shelter from the glare of the sun. Indicating she should accompany him, he showed her into the beautifully appointed clubhouse where he introduced her to the president.

'Welcome, *senorita* McLeod,' the president said and gave a formal little bow. 'I am already acquainted with your father, we met in Scotland last year.'

52

Garland had experienced a certain amount of trepidation before their meeting, but she found the president's manner quite charming. And immediately he saw her glance travel round the wall-mounted glass cases he began to tell her about the trophies they held, his English easy to understand as he named the winner of each one. She did experience one difficult moment when Nic's name was brought to her attention along with those of previous winners engraved on the base of one gleaming silver trophy.

'Now that's a player I really admire,' Simon interjected enthusiastically.

'Ah yes, but since the accident he has experienced certain difficulties,' the president told him in a hushed voice. 'Legal problems affecting his father—very sad—and I am told there was a foreigner involved.'

'Hope it doesn't affect his play,' Simon remarked, but Garland was thoughtful, wondering what Nic's legal problems could be.

On arrival, she had wondered if the players would be in the clubhouse and felt a moments trepidation in case Nic should be there, but it seemed that any players visiting the club today would be out practising on the course.

After their tour of the clubhouse they moved outside to where the presentations were to be made. The president then mentioned a few points about the introductions and line up of winners, also the place where she was to deliver her short speech. It all sounded very straightforward. Only the presence of Nic was likely to affect her emotionally, something she must strive to conceal.

Once the matter of the presentation was settled, she and Simon strolled amongst the stands to scrutinize the displays being prepared. Garland felt a surge of pride when she saw the familiar emblem of her father's firm emblazoned across the canopy and on the canvas chairs placed beneath it.

'Pity your father couldn't be here to see this for himself,' Simon remarked as they went back to the car. 'I think it's the best show we've ever put on.'

'Pity he's not here for more reasons than that,' she returned with a woeful smile, 'then my presence wouldn't be necessary.'

'Don't forget, there's the photographers to consider. The more interest we get from the media the better it will be for the firm. Besides that, I'm sure you'll make a much prettier picture than James McLeod,' he quipped.

'Don't worry, I won't quit,' she assured him as they drove away from the club. 'I'll be at the hotel tomorrow evening.'

*   *   *

A police car was pulling away from the Tropic Hotel as Garland made her way along the promenade to return to the villa that evening. Initially, on entering the house, she thought there was no-one at home until she heard Sarah moving about in her room. Feeling somewhat tired after her day in the city and the heat of the packed train carriage she decided on an early night, though it meant delaying her plan to tackle Sarah about going home until the next morning.

But Sarah's mood seemed a little subdued Garland thought as they had breakfast together on the patio the following day. Her manner wasn't exactly unpleasant, rather she appeared unusually preoccupied during the time they ate.

'There was only one car in sight as I came along the prom on my way back last night,' Garland remarked. 'It's quite unusual to see a police car here.'

Sarah's head shot up. 'Police?' she queried sharply. 'Where was that?'

'I told you, on the prom, visiting the Tropic by the look of it.'

Sarah frowned and reverted to her curiously thoughtful mood.

Thinking that maybe her sister was a trifle jealous of her attending the presentation, Garland plunged in to say, 'Are you certain you didn't want to be at the prizegiving tomorrow. After all, you usually enjoy social occasions, and you've got some fabulous dresses.'

'No fear! I have the dresses, that's true, but you know more about the firm, and you're the one with brains,' Sarah said, managing a strained smile.

'It doesn't take much brain to make a short speech, and you have lots more confidence that I do,' Garland pointed out.

'I'm not so sure,' she responded off-handedly. 'Anyway, I'm thinking of moving on, but not Edinburgh just yet.'

'Oh, Sarah, why not forget your differences with Pops and come home with me next week. You could take up acting again . . .'

Sarah tossed back her shoulder length auburn hair. 'What! Play the role of repentant daughter—oh no, he'd love that . . .'

Garland jumped to her feet. 'If you're going to start all that again, I'm going out, but when you do come to your senses let me know. I shall be leaving for Barcelona later this afternoon to prepare for tomorrow.'

Sarah raised her head, a slow smile spreading across her face. 'Tell you what, Sis, you dump your working class Romeo from the Tropic and I just might consider going back home with you.'

Determined to keep her cool, Garland returned evenly, 'That's no problem, Sarah. Working class, or any other class, he's not my Romeo, as you put it,' and without waiting for a response she left the house to go down to Pedro's. She had made up her mind, should

Nic be in the vicinity she'd ignore him rather than allow him to think his deception troubled her, or give him the pleasure of knowing she had been captivated by his charm.

Choosing a different table from the one where she'd had dinner the evening before last, she sat with her back to the road, resisting the view of the Tropic Hotel. This morning she ordered coffee, and whilst she waited for it to arrive she took the little packet of sugar from the dish to study it. Turning it over, she saw the name of the café beneath a line of palm trees printed there, reminding her of the evening she had dined here with Nic after they had strolled along the palm-fringed promenade. She felt her throat constrict with emotion and, although furious with herself for allowing the memory to affect her, she surreptitiously slid the small packet of sugar into her bag.

It was the wail of a siren that brought her out of this unhappy reverie, a siren that went suddenly silent when a car drew up somewhere behind. And when curiosity got the better of her she turned in time to catch sight of Nic dashing towards the police car which had pulled up outside the hotel. Her first thought was that someone from the hotel had suffered an accident, then she wondered if the law was after Nic because he had committed some misdemeanor. Yet, he didn't appear to be under arrest and got into the car voluntarily with the smiling policeman holding open the door. And when Pedro brought her coffee he merely responded to her enquiring glance with a typically Latin shrug.

She stirred her coffee thoughtfully. Perhaps she had been too hasty in condemning Nic— maybe he'd had good reason not to disclose his real name—he appeared a trifle anxious as he hurried towards the car. Could this be connected with the family problems the president had mentioned?

*   *   *

Nic didn't return to the hotel during the time Garland dawdled over a second cup of coffee. She felt reluctant to leave without knowing what the trouble was but realised she must soon go back to collect the items of clothing she would need for the next few days. Her evening wear was already waiting in Simon's room which meant she had less to pack, and as he had offered to drive her back on the final day, she would have no difficulty transporting her luggage. But as she set off to return to the villa, try as she may to think of only mundane things, Nic's tense expression continued to trouble her thoughts.

Sarah was nowhere to be seen when she entered the house so when the telephone rang she hurried across the sitting room to pick up the receiver.

'*Senorita* McLeod?' a male voice enquired.

'Yes, speaking,' she said and held her breath, hoping it was Nic.

'We are waiting for you to deliver . . .'

'Deliver?' she interrupted. 'I don't understand. This is Garland McLeod, who is it you wish to speak to?'

Hearing only complete silence on the line she repeated impatiently, 'Who are you—who is speaking?'

'Sorry, *senorita*, is a mistake with the number,' the caller explained in an accented voice and quickly closed the line.

Garland shrugged and returned the receiver to its rest. 'A mistake with the number?' she repeated softly. 'Somehow, I rather doubt it.' It most certainly hadn't been Nic's voice, but the caller had used the name McLeod. Had he assumed he was speaking to Sarah before he cut short his mysterious message?

*   *   *

The following morning Garland was awakened by the sound of the telephone ringing beside her bed. At first she couldn't think where she was—the window seemed to be situated at a different end of the room, there was a drone of traffic coming from outside—and it took a moment for her to collect her thoughts. Glancing at her watch as she reached for the receiver she saw it was past the time arranged

59

for breakfast, something Simon was quick to remind her when she answered the call.

Promising to be down in ten minutes, she rose and dashed into the shower. If only she had not been so late to bed this would never have happened. After a typically late dinner Simon had insisted on going through her speech, making sure she kept it short without omitting the important part which was intended to keep McLeod's name on everyone's lips. And when she had finally retired to her room sleep had evaded her until the early hours when Nic persisted in invading her thoughts.

It was almost twenty minutes later when she entered the dining room to find Simon waiting. 'You should have started without me,' she complained. 'If you hadn't kept me up so late this would never have happened.'

'Don't worry, plenty of time. I have a few matters to attend to before we leave.'

'Why must golf start at such an unearthly hour!' she grumbled as she poured her coffee. 'Surely, I shall not be expected to stand around until this evening.'

'Of course not,' he assured her with amusement. 'You can stay in the club-house until the presentation if you wish, though it would look better if you were seen to take an interest around the course. Better eat a good breakfast,' he advised, 'we're not likely to be having lunch before two in the afternoon.'

Garland took his advice and forced herself to eat another of the delicious warm rolls spread with peach conserve. Even though she dreaded what was to come, mingled with her fears was a secret surge of anticipation whenever she considered the possibility of coming face to face with Nic.

Back in her room she collected the few items she would need for the day—including her speech—and stowed them in her handbag, uttering a sad little sigh as she spotted the small packet of sugar from Pedro's. Because a warm day had been forecast, she had chosen to wear a cream dress in a crease-resistant fabric, and after a satisfied glance at her reflection her confidence was slightly restored. Closing her bag, she rang Simon to say she was ready.

*   *   *

Garland found the early morning air pleasantly fresh as she alighted from Simon's car outside the clubhouse and hesitated to view the area before they moved on towards the course. There was a smell of pines lingering on the air and she had a distant view of the sea between the trees as they walked towards the stands, past a colourful display of flags from every country taking part. She was surprised to see such activity so early in the day; gaily coloured parasols and awnings had been erected, and smiling young ladies were offering programmes to the rapidly gathering crowd.

Not far from the clubhouse, a group waited for the first team to tee off and Simon ushered her to a position where she would have a good view of play. They had not long to wait before the president made the announcement that play was about to commence and one by one he named the first team, the professional player, the celebrity cabaret star, and two players from the local club, all to loud applause. As they moved forward to tee off in turn, Garland glanced down her printed order of play to familiarise herself with the names of those taking part until Simon drew her attention to the game.

'See that, Garland—did you notice a difference in the way a professional player makes his stroke?'

Garland smiled, declining to admit she hadn't noticed a thing, but when the next team came onto the tee she tried to follow the technique of each man in turn. Between each group of players she glanced down the day's programme and her heart gave a curious jolt when she saw that Nicolau Maragall's team would be fifth to start.

'Don't we move on to the next hole now?' she asked hopefully when the third team were away.

'There's plenty of time yet,' Simon assured her. 'I would like to have a word with the president before we move on. By the way, he'll be expecting us to join his table for lunch—well, you mainly, I may be tied up at that time.'

'I'll be fine,' she insisted, hoping he would move on and allow her to stand back from this very prominent position which could put her in clear view of Nic.

'No hurry.' Simon said, adding with concern, 'Unless you want to move on before Maragall comes to the tee.'

Concealing her true feelings, she said airily, 'He doesn't worry me—as far as I'm concerned he's just another player.' Though she could feel her cheeks growing warm at the very idea of facing Nic at close quarters.

'Then you won't mind waiting for me,' he said, noting her rising colour. 'I'd like to see him tee off—he's due any minute now.'

Before Garland could make a move to conceal herself, a roar from the crowd caught her attention and there, striding onto the course came a smiling Nic, his hand raised to acknowledge the onlookers welcoming cheer. For a moment she was rooted to the spot, and before she had the presence of mind to move he had paused and was looking straight in her direction. She saw his smile fade, and for one heart-stopping moment thought he would come over to where she was standing. Instead, he merely raised his gloved hand and strode towards the tee, his smile returning.

'I'm afraid you weren't quick enough,'

Simon remarked with a wry smile as he put a consoling arm round her shoulders. 'Never mind, as you say, just think of him as another player, but watch the way he plays his stroke.'

Garland gave him a shaky little smile. 'I'll try,' she sighed and watched whilst Nic lined up the ball. With one smooth movement he brought up his club, then down with a swish of air to strike the ball, and she heard Simon's gasp of admiration as it rose way out of sight.

'See that!' Simon exclaimed, his face aglow. 'Obviously, he's been keeping in practice whilst he's been out of play.'

Garland nodded. Nic may have been keeping in practice, but not by working in a hotel, she seethed silently. Yet, furious though she was, she felt ridiculously piqued because he hadn't chosen to come over and speak to her. Unless his thoughts were elsewhere she wondered, reflecting upon his anxious expression as he'd got into the police car the day before.

CHAPTER FOUR

As soon as Nic's team had moved on, Simon took her arm and steered her through the crowd. 'I see the spectators are gathering early,' he remarked. 'They usually arrive in time to see the popular and highly-rated players start.'

'I never expected there would be so much interest,' she said looking around her. 'There must be hundreds of people already here.'

Simon laughed. 'Thousands!' he said, 'But don't worry, most people gather around the tee or the greens, it won't be quite so crowded out on the course.'

Leaving Garland at the practice green, Simon went off to speak to the president. She was delighted to see the singer from her favourite pop group practising his putting along with stage and television personalities, and men from other fields of sport. She found it entertaining to listen to the friendly banter between the players, and gradually began to feel more at ease in the pleasing outdoor atmosphere. If only she didn't have the constant distraction of Nic clouding her thoughts it could be an enjoyable day amongst the laughing crowds. She turned away, wondering if he felt any guilt about deceiving her . . .

The reappearance of Simon caught her attention and she was glad to fall in with his suggestion to visit the firm's stand. 'I'd like to see how the new lines are selling,' he said as they strolled over to the line of company stands, each with its own trade name emblazoned across the front.

At the sight of McLeod's logo she experienced a little surge of pride, noting that it stood out amongst the others, and the immaculately dressed members of staff were already busily attending to interested buyers. The future looked good for McLeod's. If only her own could be so rosy she thought with a sad little sigh.

Satisfied with the stand, Simon suggested they walk the course, and it was almost two hours later when they crossed the well-kept fairway at the seventh that she realised they could be catching up with Nic Maragall's team.

'It's so hot, Simon and I'm really thirsty. Can we get a drink somewhere?'

'Of course,' he agreed. 'There's a bar-tent near the ninth green, we can watch play from there.'

Garland wondered how far Nic would have got by the time they reached the ninth and was relieved when Simon led her away from the area of play, cutting across between the trees towards the refreshment tent. Perhaps if she hurried her drink they could move on before Nic reached the ninth hole. But she wasn't the only thirsty spectator and service was slow so that when the sound of applause reached Simon's ears he ushered her back outside towards the green.

'Must be someone of note,' he said, urging her forward, 'maybe that pop star you've been raving about. Let's see if I can find you a good viewing place.'

The area around the green was already

crowded with spectators though Garland assured him she could see quite well. But she quickly ducked from view when she caught sight of Nic, his red shirt and navy blue slacks clearly visible as he advanced towards the green where he hesitated, appearing to scan the crowd.

Simon nudged her. 'Watch this—he has a putt of about two metres.' And Garland raised her head a fraction to watch as Nic concentrated on his shot.

'Brilliant—perfect balance!' Simon exclaimed as the ball rolled straight towards the hole and disappeared. 'They're four under already.'

'Under what?' she asked innocently as they returned to the refreshment tent.

'Didn't your father teach you anything?' he asked in mock despair as they moved towards the bar. 'It means they've reached the ninth hole four strokes under the number allowed for that distance.'

'Oh, I see,' she murmured softly. 'Then whoever gets round with the least number of strokes wins—is that it?'

'You've got the idea,' he laughed. 'In fact, I'll take you to have a shot on the practice green later.'

'I'm not so sure about that,' she said, wrinkling her nose. She was finding the game quite fascinating, yet doubted she could match the skill required.

Somewhat to her relief, at each fairway and green they visited after leaving the tent, Nic's team stayed a short distance ahead. She had experienced a curious feeling of elation from watching him play; the muscular line of his body as he made his shots, and the accuracy of his game were curiously stimulating and she became almost disappointed not to have caught up with his team. And when Simon suggested it was time to join the president at lunch, Nic was still out on the course.

*   *   *

'My money's on Maragall's team,' Simon was saying to the president as they took their seats in the dining room.

'You could be right!' the president agreed. 'Quite frankly, I was beginning to fear he'd abandoned the game altogether after the problems he experienced as a result of the accident earlier this year . . .'

He broke off as an official came over, but already Garland's curiosity had been aroused. 'What problems is he speaking of?' she whispered to Simon.

'No idea. I believe I mentioned the accident, when he was struck by a car,' he continued. 'Evidently, it took him a while to recover from his injuries but the vehicle didn't stop so they were unable to prove anything against the driver.'

'For someone in his profession that would come as quite a blow,' she agreed, still quietly curious as to what the other problem could have been. Was it in any way connected with his visit from the police? Had he also allowed them to believe he was on the staff of the Tropic Hotel?

She suddenly realised the president was looking at her, his brows raised. 'I'm sorry,' she said quickly, 'were you speaking to me?'

'I was asking if you are enjoying the game,' he repeated politely, 'though I am sure you would find it very warm out on the course.'

Equally politely Garland responded, and the light conversation, interspersed with a little golf talk, went on throughout the lengthy meal. When they went back on the course, Nic's team had already reached the eighteenth with a score well under par.

'What a come-back!' cried Simon with unfailing admiration. 'With that score, I reckon his team are the winners.'

Garland groaned inwardly. This was going to be the moment she dreaded and, unconsciously, she straightened her shoulders. She couldn't let her father down, so when the time came to hand over the prize she would fix her eyes on something beyond Nic rather than meet his dark-eyed gaze.

Simon appeared a trifle anxious when the time for the prize giving arrived, but Garland braced herself, assuring him she could cope.

There, in front of the club-house, a small group lined up behind a table draped in velvet with the cut glass rose bowl displayed upon it, plus sets of equipment manufactured by McLeod's. But there was no sign of Nic. No doubt he would make his entrance when he was announced she surmised as the president beckoned her forward.

Her heart seemed to increase its beating as she went towards the table but she managed a wide smile to acknowledge the welcoming applause following the president's announcement. She was relieved to note that Simon was close at hand so that when the president had finished speaking he was able to prompt her when it was her turn to speak.

Taking a deep breath, she delivered her short speech on behalf of McLeod's and prepared to make the presentation. But she was quite unprepared for the disappointment she felt when the president announced that, in the absence of *senor* Maragall, another member of the team would accept the prize on their behalf. Had Nic known she would be at the presentation? she wondered. Had he deliberately set out to avoid her? This awful feeling of anticlimax brought unexpected tears to her eyes and she had to fight against the almost overwhelming emotion.

*   *   *

'The President informed me Maragall left the course after he'd posted his score, but he didn't give a reason,' Simon told her as they drove back to the hotel.

'It didn't make the slightest difference to the prize-giving,' she managed casually, though had she known beforehand it would have eased the tension. 'However, I did have the opportunity to exchange a couple of words with the pop singer I simply rave about—I was really pleased about that.'

'I suppose that would make it all worthwhile,' he responded with a grin. 'You seemed very much on edge beforehand.'

She gave a shaky little laugh. 'Oh dear, am I so transparent—whatever will I be like at the final?'

'You'll cope,' he assured her. 'Right now I'm looking forward to a shower and change of clothes. We're not meeting until nine so there's plenty of time to relax before dinner.'

Back at the hotel, Garland decided to rest a while before she got ready for the evening. But she hadn't realised how tired she had been until she switched on the TV and noticed the time, discovering she'd slept for more than an hour. But as soon as the screen came to life she was immediately alert. It was the sports report, and although she wasn't familiar with the language the picture on the screen was very clear. There, dressed in the unmistakable red shirt and navy trousers, was Nic about to play his final shot at the eighteenth. Mesmerized, she watched him putt the ball with perfect accuracy, saw his triumphant smile as he raised his arms to acknowledge the roar of the crowd. And when the programme moved on she stayed glued to the screen, only coming back to the present at the scene of the presentation when she was pleased to note her few words in the language of the region went down reasonably well. But even after the programme ended she found it impossible to relax, the picture of Nic still bothering her. And all the while she bathed and dressed her thoughts kept drifting back so that by the time she selected her outfit for the evening she had made the decision to confront him when the next opportunity arose. She had to know why he concealed his identity and what purpose he expected it to serve.

*   *   *

When she and Simon entered the club bar that evening the guests were already moving towards the dining room and she felt obliged to offer an apology.

'Is no problem,' the president assured her, casting an appreciative glance over the emerald silk outfit she was wearing before the dining room manager directed them to their seats.

Garland found herself seated between the

president and his wife, with Simon sitting opposite. To her dismay, the lady spoke no English so she had to rely on her own few polite phrases to initiate a little conversation. But, surprisingly, Simon seemed to be coping with the language reasonably well and it was a relief to leave him to do most of the talking while they waited for the meal to be served.

Sipping a glass of dry, sparkling wine, she glanced along the head table to see a few faces she recalled from earlier in the day, including the celebrity and the local amateur players from the winning team. But, as she expected, Nic was not present which would account for the empty place beside the president's wife. In one way, she was thankful for his absence; she needed somewhere more private when she challenged him, otherwise her courage may fail.

This evening everyone appeared to be in a celebratory mood, and Simon appeared to be getting along famously with others seated at their table. The first course was a dainty selection of seafood, which Garland enjoyed, and she was about to comment on it when she noticed Simon looking in her direction, his expression strangely apprehensive. She then became aware that the hubbub of voices around her had fallen silent, only to rise again in an unexpected burst of applause. Glancing up she saw Nic, now formally dressed, advancing towards the head table, his eyes meeting hers briefly as he greeted their hosts and seated himself at the *senora's* side. Lowering her eyes, her glance rested on Simon who visibly relaxed when she managed to send him a smile. She was aware of the president waving aside Nic's apology when he explained that he had experienced a delay on his journey here. And by the *senora's* response Garland knew, in their eyes, Nicolau Maragall could do no wrong.

After this the remainder of the meal seemed to lose its appeal for her and she toyed with every course. Keeping her eyes on her plate she listened to the conversation Simon was having with the president and the celebrity of the winning team until the *senora* caught her attention to enquire if she had been introduced to *senor* Maragall.

'Er, yes, I . . .' she began falteringly as she met Nic's cool stare at which she inwardly recoiled.

'*Si si*, I made this young lady's acquaintance before the competition,' Nic supplied smoothly in their own language. Repeating it in English, he added, 'Even so, I did not expect to find her here today.'

'Had I known you would be here I might have changed my plans,' she retaliated, forcing a smile, and caught his sharp glance.

'I'm so pleased you decided against it,' he said softly, 'as I think you owe me an explanation.'

'I owe you an explanation!' she returned in an equally low voice as she cast an uncomfortable glance in the direction of the president's smiling wife. 'I think you are mistaken, *senor*.'

'I consider it would be extremely discourteous to our hosts if we continue this conversation,' he said, his tone faintly arrogant as he returned his attention to the *senora* when he reverted to their own tongue.

Garland subsided into an annoyed silence. How dare he suggest she be at fault! What kind of explanation did he expect? This man was the limit!

It took a great deal of effort on her part to gather the thread of conversation around her and only Simon's expression of sheer enjoyment helped her to relax.

'I'm in for a really busy time!' he leaned forward to whisper. 'The President has offered me a game before I go back, and I hope to have a word with today's winner before the evening is over.'

'Then I wish you luck!' said Garland a trifle acidly, aware that Nic's eyes still rested upon her.

Seeing he had caught Nic Maragall's attention, Simon immediately broke into Spanish when it sounded to Garland as though they were having a most agreeable conversation. And as the president rose to make his speech she thought she understood

Nic to signal that he wished to continue his conversation with Simon afterwards.

Thankfully, the president's speech was short, though Simon had warned her they were usually the opposite. He congratulated the winners, thanked everyone attending, and spoke a little about the championship to be played over the next few days, then resumed his seat after announcing the dancing was about to begin. And when spotlights were focused on a trio in one corner of the room the president rose to his feet and took her hand, inviting her to dance.

Knowing it would be discourteous to refuse, she allowed him to lead her to the small dance-floor, nervously aware of the attention focused upon her. But the president danced in a very relaxed manner, chatting amiably as they moved round the floor. She saw Simon was partnering the president's wife and glanced to where Nic was sitting, a cigar between his fingers as he gazed indolently around the room. And when the music started up again with a slow Latin melody, she gladly accepted her favourite pop star's invitation to dance. But, disappointingly, he proved to be devoid of charm, his manner quite boastful, and she was relieved when the next request came from Simon.

'Enjoying yourself?' he asked as they moved slowly round the floor.

'Yes, of course,' she lied, 'though I won't be

content until I've given your hero a piece of my mind.'

'Why upset yourself and spoil a good time?' he whispered, weaving skillfully between the other dancers. 'Actually, Garland, you're looking particularly dishy this evening, and I'm not the only one to notice.'

She looked up at him in surprise. 'Thank you, Simon,' she responded with a smile, but her expression froze when he released his hold on her and Nic took her firmly in his arms.

'It seems that this is the only way I'm going to make contact with you tonight,' he said. 'But I'm determined you're going to explain why you didn't tell me about your connection with McLeod's.'

'And what about you?' she retaliated. 'You allowed me believe you were a waiter at the Tropic.'

'No,' he corrected her, 'you presumed I was, though I must confess it amused me at the time . . .'

'Amusing yourself at my expense,' she shot back, lowering her voice a little when she realised a couple nearby were sending them curious looks.

'Of course not,' he declared. 'When we last met I was about to make a confession about my real position in the hotel. But if you remember, not wishing to change the mood of the evening, you interrupted me. Then I received a rather urgent telephone call so I lost the opportunity to put things right.'

On reflection, Garland did remember him saying there was something more serious he wished to discuss, but she hadn't wanted to spoil the happy moment and had presumed it to be a matter of little importance when he'd hurried away.

'You must believe me, Garland,' he continued when she didn't reply. 'It wasn't my intention to deceive you, though I now realise I should have connected your name with today's event.' As he spoke his grip on her hand tightened. She wanted to believe him more than anything, but . . .

'And now, what is your excuse?' he queried with a grim smile as he manoeuvred her expertly round the small dance floor. 'I would have thought an occasion such as this deserved a mention.'

'Actually, I didn't know I would be here until my father telephoned two days ago, and you may remember that you didn't appear exactly ecstatic when I told you I would be staying another week.'

'But you didn't say why, even when you left that message at the hotel,' he chided her gently. 'I was so disappointed because I knew I wouldn't be there and you now know the reason. But if only you had told me . . .' He broke off and drew her closer to murmur against her hair, 'Oh, Garland, what fools we have been.'

'I know,' she whispered with a surge of relief and felt his lips brush her forehead. And when the rhythm changed she willingly agreed to Nic's suggestion that they take a stroll outside.

The sound of music had faded by the time they reached the trees bordering the course where the scent of pines hung heavily on the still night air. And as they walked hand in hand she explained the reason she had been asked to make the presentations.

'I'm mainly involved in design, so I'm not always aware of what my father's plans are,' she told him. 'You have no idea how terrified I was when he asked me to stand in for his partner.'

'According to the president, you managed very well. Pity I had to miss it.'

'Then it was not intentional? I did wonder as you didn't look particularly pleased to see me earlier today.'

'No, Garland, I was not displeased, but you must realise it came as quite a shock. I had to attend a rather important appointment in the city this evening, but I was determined to get back in time for dinner in the hope you'd be here.'

As he spoke those last few words he drew her into his arms and Garland felt her heartbeat quicken. And when he tilted her chin, compelling her to look up at him, her lips parted in anticipation.

But he didn't attempt to kiss her as she had

expected. Instead, he held her gaze for a moment, his dark brow raised questioningly as he enquired, 'Tell me, how does this evening compare with the glitzy night-life Meredith enjoys?'

The mere mention of Don sent her heart plummeting. 'Please, don't even mention him,' she begged with a shudder. 'He's someone I'd rather forget.'

'Of course, forgive me,' he murmured, and cupping her face in his hands, he sought to capture her mouth and her hands slid up to encircle his neck as the pressure of his lips increased.

'Garland,' he murmured as their lips drew apart, 'I must see you again. Maybe tomorrow night?'

'I shall be at the course in the morning,' she reminded him in a slightly breathless voice, 'and I'll be here for the remainder of the week.'

'But I'll be involved in the game during the day,' he complained. 'Promise me you will keep your evenings free.'

'Yes, Nic, of course,' she agreed. 'Simon is usually around during play, and he explains the game to me so I'm finding it quite enjoyable.'

'Perhaps you will allow me to teach you how to play now you are beginning to enjoy it,' he suggested, and after a slight hesitation added, 'unless that is Simon's prerogative?'

Garland smiled. 'Hardly,' she said, 'Simon is merely a colleague. Until now, we have met only in the office. And, unless he's already mentioned it, I know he'd give anything for a round of golf with you.'

'I'd be delighted,' he agreed, 'but first there is tomorrow evening—perhaps we could have dinner in town, then a tour of the popular areas in the centre of the city. Would you like that?'

'Oh yes, I'd love it, providing it's not too late, you may have to make an early start the day after.'

'Don't worry, I'm drawn to tee off at ten the following day so it is not too late for me. We will, as you say in your country, paint the town red—yes?' he smiled, and they turned to stroll back towards the bright lights and the sound of music.

Garland laughed. She felt as though she was walking on air, when even her anxiety over the presentation ceased to be a matter of concern. And when they entered the clubhouse he slid a possessive arm round her waist and led her back to the dance-floor, gently guiding her into the evocative rhythm of a rumba.

Garland had never considered herself to be a particularly good dancer but in Nic's arms she felt light-footed and perfectly able to follow his lead. And she had to smile when she spotted Simon taking the floor for the last dance, his brows raised speculatively as he caught her eye.

*   *   *

'For someone who wanted to avoid Maragall at all cost, you didn't do too well,' Simon teased as they drove back to the hotel. 'What happened to change your mind?'

'Merely a slight misunderstanding between us,' she told him with a secretive smile, 'nothing more.'

'Well, it's certainly cheered you up!' he said bluntly. 'And, thanks to you, he's giving me a game. By the way, did you find out what the trouble was he'd experienced recently?'

'No, I must admit I didn't like to ask, and he never offered to tell me,' she replied, then fell silent as they sped through the darkness, her thoughts dwelling on Nic. He had offered to drive her back to her hotel, but she had felt obliged to return with Simon as he had brought her. She glanced across to find him concentrating on the road ahead, his fair skin rosy from his day in the sun. Dear Simon, she thought, he had been a perfect escort throughout the long day even though he'd had his own side of the business to attend to.

'We never had the chance to dance again,' she commented. 'I hope you didn't mind Nic interrupting so soon after we had taken the floor.'

'The original dumb blond,' he murmured

with a chuckle. 'Had you not realised? Nic was desperate for an opportunity to talk to you so we had that already planned.'

'Oh, Simon, I ought to have known!' she cried then, with a sigh of contentment, added, 'But I'm glad you did so you're forgiven.'

Simon grinned in the darkness, then remembered Nic had made a rather unusual enquiry regarding Garland and her sister. 'Oh yes, there was something else he mentioned—he was quite serious, and persistent—he wanted to know if you came to Spain by plane, or if either you or your sister had made the journey by car?'

CHAPTER FIVE

The first day of the tournament dawned with a cloudless sky and the promise of good weather on the course. Remembering the heat of the previous day she chose to wear the lightest outfit she had brought with her, teamed with flat sandals that would be easier on her feet. As usual, Simon was down early for breakfast and today she made a special effort to join him.

'Would you mind dining alone this evening, Simon?' she asked once seated at the table.

'Of course not,' he said, but his lips quirked mischievously as he went on to enquire, 'Will you be dining with Nic Maragall by any chance?'

'He has invited me, but I feel a little guilty about deserting you.'

'Don't worry, Garland, I expect the sales staff will be around. Anyway, I'm pleased to hear you two are on friendly terms again.'

She was just about to pour a second cup of coffee when she was called to the telephone in reception. Assuming it would be her father, she was surprised to hear Sarah on the line, her voice faintly hysterical.

'When will you be back?' her sister demanded. 'I hate it here on my own.'

'But you're all right?' Garland queried, recovering from her surprise. 'You're not ill or anything, are you?'

'Not really, but I'm terribly lonely . . .' was Sarah's mournful response.

Garland gave a short laugh. 'That's a bit dramatic, what's got into you? Won't your friend Patricia be keeping you company?'

'She and I are no longer friends,' Sarah announced. 'I've asked her not to call here again.'

'You do surprise me, Sarah. Personally, I never did care for the woman.'

Garland was about to ask if Don Meredith had called but thought better of it. Instead she reminded her sister, 'You know, you're going to be even more lonely when I'm back in Edinburgh.'

'I've been thinking about that,' she admitted. 'If only you were here, we could discuss it . . .'

'Sorry Sis, I must go, Simon's waiting, but we'll discuss it when this tournament is over. Meanwhile, read a book or go for a walk, it will help to pass the time.'

Sarah seemed to hesitate before she blurted out, 'I've been thinking of ringing Mark. He gave me his mobile number when we last spoke—begged me to let him join me in Spain—said he would soon be leaving for his place in the south of France which is not too far from here.'

'It's a pity you broke off your engagement, he was such fun and he thought the world of you.'

'I know,' Sarah agreed brokenly. 'I deeply regret our parting. It was stupid of me, I realise that now.'

'It's a bit late for that. Perhaps now you will appreciate what you've lost.'

'Oh I do—if only he would give me another chance . . .'

'Perhaps I ought to warn him!' Garland teased until she heard Sarah's cry of protest. 'Don't worry, I'll ring you later—I promise—but now I really must go.'

Simon had finished his breakfast by the time she returned to the dining room. 'Everything all right?' he queried, noting her thoughtful expression.

'Everything's fine,' she said with a vague smile. 'It was only my sister.'

'There's nothing wrong is there? You look serious.'

'No, Simon, she's just feeling lonely without me—much to my surprise! I'll ring her when we get back. That should keep her happy, though I suspect she's merely being over dramatic. She's an actress you see—or was until a few months ago—always inclined to exaggerate'

'I see, but if there's anything I can do you will ask?'

She nodded. 'Actually, there is. If my father should get in touch with you don't tell him there's anything amiss. He'll only worry.'

'Fine, if that is what you want,' he said, sending her a quizzical glance as they left the dining room to go to his car.

Once they reached the course Simon went off to discuss the display stand with his staff. From her programme, Garland saw that Nic wasn't due to tee off for another half an hour so she left Simon chatting and went across to the first hole to watch the early players. Then, not wishing Nic to have the impression she was only waiting for him to appear, she continued round the course with the early team. Today the play was more serious, none of the humorous banter of the previous day; there was quite a large sum of money at stake in the final and each man's concentration was intense.

Eventually Simon caught up with her and directed her attention back along the course when she spotted the unmistakable figure of Nic striding along the fairway. She paused long enough to watch him take a powerful drive at the ball, lifting it high over the trees to land on the tenth green. From the distant cry of the spectators she guessed the shot had been well aimed. Moving ahead, pausing occasionally to watch play, she kept hearing the name Maragall amongst the buzz of the spectators' conversation and had to struggle against the urge to wait for him to catch up when she could savour his every move for herself.

By the time Nic had reached the eighteenth green Garland had made sure she was in a position where her view would not be obscured. And when he came to take his final putt she saw his expression was tense with concentration. Inadvertently, she clenched her fists as she watched, her eyes fixed on the ball, willing it to reach the hole. She heard the click as the club made contact and was just in time to see Nic raise his arm in a gesture of triumph before she was caught up in the surge of delighted spectators.

'Thought I'd find you here,' Simon said. 'I think Nic was looking for you in the crowd.'

'I couldn't get anywhere near, everybody was so excited it was impossible to get through.'

'He may soon be leaving the course—want me to find him for you?'

'No need, thanks, we've already made arrangements. He's picking me up at the hotel at half past eight so I won't bother him now.'

'Terrific!' said Simon as they went in the direction of the official car park. 'Incidentally, where's he staying?'

Pausing, she turned to look at him. 'Strange you should mention it, I've no idea, but I'll ask him tonight. Up to now he's not been very forthcoming so I may learn very little.' And in response to Simon's expression of disbelief she disclosed, 'You may not believe it but he's a rather secretive sort of person.'

*   *   *

Promptly at half past eight the phone rang in Garland's room to announce Nic's arrival, and going down to reception she found him studying the evening paper.

'I hope you will excuse me for a moment,' she said, indicating the booth nearby. 'I need to telephone my sister again, I couldn't get a reply earlier.'

But although she kept the phone ringing for longer than usual, as with the call she'd made on her return from the course, there still was no response. Sarah must have taken her advice and gone out walking, or perhaps she was having dinner at the Tropic Hotel.

With a shrug she returned to where Nic waited. 'I'll try again later,' she said, replacing her slightly troubled expression with a smile.

'You can use my mobile if you wish,' he offered.

'Thanks, I may take you up on that, mine needs charging.'

Outside the hotel, beside the busy tree-lined road, he paused to say, 'I thought you may like to see the city at night, providing you are not too tired after being on the course all day.'

'Oh yes, I would. And I'd like to see the flower stalls further along the *Rambla*. It looks so lively and colourful.'

He laughed and took her hand. 'It will be very crowded, but if you stay close to me I won't lose you.'

Content to stay as close as possible she smiled up at him and said, 'I'm pleased to be staying in a central hotel, it enables me to do a little sightseeing. How about you, are you staying in the city, or do you drive back to the Tropic every night?'

'Not every day,' he replied, guiding her between the traffic over to the central walkway. 'Ah, it is better here, not quite so crowded.'

Determined to pin him down, she said, 'I suppose it will save you travelling. Are you staying anywhere near here?'

'Not too far away,' he told her off-handedly, and as if wanting to change the subject enquired, 'Are you very hungry, or shall we call somewhere for an aperitif?'

'Yes, I'd like that. It's still quite warm so maybe we can sit outside?'

'Of course. There is a square on the left—*Placa Real*, ideal for people watching—and tomorrow evening we can continue our tour down to the port.'

'I'd like to see as much as possible whilst I'm here,' she agreed, pleased to hear he intended to meet her socially again.

'You never know, you may come back next year if your father is sponsoring the tournament,' he suggested, his dark brows raised questioningly as he steered her off the busy main street towards the square.

'At least I wouldn't be so nervous,' she laughed as they seated themselves at a table in the open air, 'though perhaps my sister can be persuaded to do the presentation next time.'

'I'd prefer you to be there,' he said softly, causing Garland to smile.

'Anything could happen before next year,' she said, a faint tremor in her voice. 'I'm not even sure if the villa will still be ours. My father rarely has the time to come here, and my sister may have tired of it by then.'

'You're so different from your sister. I don't just mean in looks or the colour of your hair, more in personality,' he remarked, adding thoughtfully, 'Yes, if she had your character she would not be frittering her time away here.'

Garland was taken aback. 'How can you say that, you don't even know her.'

'Perhaps I know more than you realise,' he returned cryptically, his eyes darkly brooding.

'You do? Ah well, I suppose the hotel will be a hive of gossip, and lies,' she returned crossly.

Nic laughed, a rather harsh sound. 'I think lying is the prerogative of your sister and her friend.'

Hurt by his insidious remarks, she said coolly, 'I'm afraid you're out of touch, I understand they are no longer friends.'

'So all they now share is the colour of their hair,' he stated. 'Your sister will be a wiser woman, though it will mean drastic changes in her way of life.'

'Do I detect a note of criticism of my sister's lifestyle?'

'Garland, you have no idea of her lifestyle,' he said and drew in a long breath. 'And I doubt she will enlighten you if you ask . . .'

'True. Like you, she's not exactly forthcoming. Even the simplest question is met with a cool silence.'

He shook his head and sighed, 'I'm sorry, Garland, I'd like to rectify that.'

'I'll admit it's none of my business,' she said, 'yet, if I recall, you knew my name the day we first met and you asked me some quite personal questions.'

'I agree, I did, and now perhaps you will allow me to explain why . . .'

'It's almost as though you don't trust me,' she interrupted, 'and I doubt if you would have revealed your true identity if we hadn't met on the course.'

'Indeed I would, particularly now I know you are the daughter of the firm of McLeod.'

'Ah yes, I remember, you know my father.'

'We first met in Portugal when I was new at the game, then Scotland.'

'But why did you need to be convinced of who I am? Or is that another question you will avoid answering?'

'Certainly not, but it would mean involving you in something which could distress you, and something I may later regret.'

'Distress me?' she queried, frowning. 'Unless you tell me I won't know if I find it distressing or not.'

He uttered a long sigh. 'Ah, Garland, it is a very complicated situation,' he said softly. 'It involves Meredith with whom you appeared to be on friendly terms—that is, both you and your sister.'

'I find the mere mention of the name Meredith distressing,' she told him, 'particularly when it is connected with my sister and me.'

'Forgive me, at first I was confused, but now you can assure me the connection with Meredith has been severed I trust you implicitly.'

As Nic spoke, she became aware of his warm hand seeking hers where it rested on the table, the faintly caressing fingers titillating her senses. And it was a moment before she could gather her thoughts to suggest, 'Perhaps you'd better tell me about Meredith. Obviously, it seems there's even more to his character than I was aware.'

Nic took a long breath and gripped her hand more firmly. 'He is an absolute rogue,' he stated grimly, 'and someone who caused much suffering in my family by his deception.' He gave a slow shake of his head as he went on to say, 'He was never personally involved as, apart from the Blanford woman, he used the more gullible to implement his racket.'

'What sort of racket are you speaking of?' she asked, momentarily startled. Whatever she had thought of Don, she hadn't expected to hear this.

'Ah, it is a long story, and as you are no longer involved with Meredith there is little to be gained by repeating it,' he said with a dismissive lift of his shoulders.

'Oh, Nic, you arouse my interest and then you refuse to tell me . . .'

He laughed and placed a finger lightly on her lips. 'What was it you said to me when we dined in Pedro's—let us not be serious and spoil our evening together?'

She shot him a rueful smile. 'Yes, I

remember, was it anything important?'

'I think I was about to admit to my true position, but you were right, such happy occasions are too precious to spoil.'

'I agree, but even so, I ought to warn my sister. There's a possibility she could be with him right now.'

He took his mobile phone from his pocket. 'Here, no need to go into detail, just advise her to keep away from Meredith, and his club, or she may find herself in serious trouble.'

'Perhaps then you will tell me what this is about,' she said as she keyed in the number. Minutes passed and she uttered a deep sigh as she handed back the phone. 'Still no reply, I'll try again later.'

'We must hope she is not with Meredith, or the Blanford woman before you have the opportunity to speak to her.' Noting Garland's anxious expression he reached for her hand. 'Try not to let it worry you.'

'Oh, Nic, I can't help it, my sister can be such an idiot! I've warned her a number of times . . .'

'You have warned her?' he broke in. 'For what reason?'

'Oh, different things,' she murmured turning away to avoid the intensity of his dark stare. 'For instance, I noticed she was paying for Patricia Blanford's meals and taxis, amongst other things. It was almost as if my sister couldn't refuse, she was nervous in her company and seemed to give in to her every whim. I intend to tackle her about it.'

He sighed. 'I think you've missed your opportunity, Patricia Blanford appears to have disappeared from the area. The problem is, no-one can prove anything against her, even though the police had her under observation.'

'Oh, I hadn't realised . . .' Garland began then, recalling what Nic had said a short time before, prompted him, 'You haven't yet told me what this is about.'

He let out a slow breath before going on to say, 'In my father's case it was the Blanford woman who lied her way out of trouble. Some months ago, as he and I walked back to the Tropic Hotel from the local golf club, we were involved in an accident. Unfortunately, I didn't manage to get out of the way in time to avoid being struck by a car traveling at high speed. As a result I was taken to hospital with concussion and a few broken ribs which, as you may guess, is hardly conducive to my profession.'

'How awful for you,' she said, and supposed this was the accident Simon had spoken of. 'Did it take you long to recover?'

'Not really as I'm quite fit and healthy, but my poor father still suffers even though he was uninjured after I managed to pull him out of the path of the car.'

'The shock I should think. But tell me, in what way is Patricia Blanford connected with this?'

'Because that woman was at the wheel, my father saw her, but she has denied everything,' he said, ending emphatically. 'He is elderly, but not senile, so I know he is right. In fact, I have yet to meet a man more capable at his age.'

'She shouldn't have been allowed to get away with it,' Garland declared. 'Were the police not called in?'

'Yes, but nothing could be proved against her, she had the perfect alibi, and so that devious woman escaped prosecution.'

'Oh, I see,' Garland said thoughtfully. 'But if your father saw her, surely her alibi wouldn't hold water.'

'As I said, she is an extremely devious woman. She insisted she had an appointment with her hairdresser in the city at that time. The owner of the business confirmed this, but I think she persuaded someone else to take her place, but using her name.'

Garland's eyes widened. 'But if she had regular appointments her hairdresser would recognise it wasn't her, wouldn't he?'

Nic gave a bitter smile. 'Not if a replacement was used every time, just think how often such an alibi could be used.'

'I hadn't thought of that,' she admitted. 'Your father must have found it very frustrating, particularly if he was convinced she was driving.'

'Oh yes, he had seen her in the hotel very often—he is the proprietor, you see—he couldn't have been mistaken.'

'And do you think Don Meredith is somehow involved as well as that woman?'

'I'm convinced he is, both with that and other lucrative but illegal matters.'

'Thank goodness I no longer feature in his life,' she declared with an involuntary shudder. 'I've had a narrow escape,'

'Do you find it cold?' he asked. We can move on if you are ready.'

'No, it just makes me shudder to think I've ever been in his company,' she said with an expression of distaste. Brightening again, she smiled at him. 'However, I may not be cold but I am beginning to feel quite hungry.'

He gave her a rueful smile. 'Forgive me, I am forgetting that you dine much earlier in your own country.'

'I suppose I would get used to your hours eventually, given time here to adjust.'

'Do you think you could grow to like being here once you had adjusted to our lifestyle and habits?'

She pursed her lips, then said thoughtfully, 'I have mixed feelings. Part of me enjoys the hours of sunshine and so many wonderful things to see . . .'

'And the other part of you?' he pressed as they rose from the table.

'That part remembers my responsibilities,'

she told him with a sigh, 'and the fact I was here initially to persuade my sister to go back home.'

'The divided heart,' he murmured softly as he took her hand, guiding her between the strollers towards a restaurant.

'This restaurant is called The Snails,' he told her as they waited to be shown to a table, and indicating the busy open kitchen observed with a smile, 'Though the speed they work can hardly be described as a snail's pace.'

Garland wrinkled her nose. 'But I don't have to eat snails, do I?'

He laughed and shook his head. 'Not if you do not wish, but you can always try one of mine.'

The head waiter showed them to a table on the mezzanine floor overlooking the busy area around the kitchen and cash desk. Garland thought it fascinating and gazed around at the assortment of bottles on the shelves, the smoke cured hams, and bunches of dried herbs hanging from the darkened ceiling.

'It's all so unusual,' she said, looking over the rail to view the scene below where chefs juggled food in very hot pans and waiters dashed back and forth bearing a plate on one forearm and another in each hand.

'I was sure you would like to see this place and try a few regional dishes . . .' he began, but before he could continue she nudged his hand to draw his attention to the trio standing by the cash desk on the ground floor.

'Nic! Look—yes, it's her! It's Patricia!' she gasped, spotting the woman's shining auburn hair.

Nic leaned forward. 'Ah, so it is, and it looks as though they are about to leave. Do you recognise the men with her?'

Garland studied the two men, the younger one impatiently drumming his fingers on the cash desk as they waited for the Blanford woman to pay the bill. 'I don't recall seeing them before,' she whispered. 'Have you?'

'They don't appear to be British,' he commented softly. 'And I'm relieved to see your sister is not with them, particularly as you received no reply when you telephoned earlier.'

'For a moment, when I saw the auburn hair, I thought it was Sarah,' she admitted, then nudged him again. 'Nic, look, they're taking a parcel of food away with them!'

'I believe meals can be purchased for those who prefer to dine at home,' he said, then seeing Patricia's upward glance as she made to leave he quickly drew Garland back into the shadow of the herbs and hams, out of the other woman's view.

She cast Nic a worried glance. 'I wonder where she's going now?'

'Providing it is not in our vicinity, I don't really care,' he said with a shrug. 'So, let us forget about them and give our attention to the menu. I can't wait to see you tackle one of those snails they are cooking down below.'

Meeting his teasing smile Garland declared, 'I'm not exactly relishing the thought.' And although the conversation remained light between them, she couldn't fail to notice a slight tension in his manner, and found her eyes straying to the lower floor more than once though she doubted Patricia would return.

'Hey, don't forget you wanted to try one of these,' he reminded her once she had finished her main course, and he passed the ceramic dish containing a single snail across the table before topping up her glass with wine.

'Ugh, I couldn't!' she cried laughingly. 'I'm sure I saw it move.'

'And I always thought the Scots were a brave race,' he joked. 'Obviously, I was mistaken.'

'Perhaps another time, Nic,' she said, twirling her wineglass in her fingers.

His dark eyes searched hers as he reached for her hand. 'I'm so pleased to hear there will be another time. Will you meet me again tomorrow evening?'

'I'd like that,' she murmured, then seeing no-one was seated nearby asked, 'I'd like to use your mobile again, if you don't mind?'

Nic keyed in the number before handing her the phone, meeting the look of surprise on her face. 'I know that number as well as I do my own,' he explained.

But Garland's smile began to fade when the mobile continued to ring, unanswered. 'Are you sure you have the right number?'

He nodded, indicating she try it herself, but still without success. 'Maybe she has gone out for the evening,' he said noting her worried expression. 'I am sure she will have other friends in the neighbourhood.'

'I've not heard her mention anyone in particular but I suppose it's possible. I'll ring from the hotel later—she should be back by then.'

'I'm sure you are right, don't worry. Now, what will you have for dessert?'

'Just coffee for me, please.'

'Shall we share a portion of fruit and nuts? In the past, they were given to the musicians who entertained so there's a tradition attached to this dish.'

He was about to continue when a flower seller came to their table. Taking one of the individually wrapped red rosebuds he said softly, 'Another tradition—a beautiful rose is a token of love on Saint George's day.' And as he handed her the long-stemmed rose a gentle smile flickered on his sensuous mouth.

Garland was delighted by this gesture and closed her eyes as she held it to her nose to catch its perfume. And though it had a most heavenly scent, its colour reminded her of Patricia Blanford's pouting ruby lips each time she had tried to inveigle her way into Sarah's favour.

'Thank you, I think it's a lovely tradition,' she said, opening her eyes to shake off the memory of Patricia.

CHAPTER SIX

As they left the restaurant Nic linked his arm through hers, pausing a moment in the shadows of a quiet square to tell her how much he had enjoyed the evening. As he drew her into his arms Garland felt her heartbeat quicken, and when he tilted her chin so that she was looking into his eyes, her lips parted slightly in anticipation.

But he didn't attempt to kiss her. Instead, he held her in close regard, his dark brow raised questioningly as he enquired, 'Tell me, Garland, what type of employment did Meredith have to offer?'

'Oh, Nic, why must you keep mentioning his name? I'm tired of hearing it.'

'You and many others—particularly those who were subjected to his intimidation where employment is concerned.' He compressed his lips a moment before he added, 'Your apparent lack of concern surprises me.'

Lowering her head she admitted in a barely audible voice, 'I didn't mean it like that. I'm sure you're right . . .'

'Then why avoid the question?' he persisted, drawing her back to face him.

'It's just . . . well, it has become more than just a personal issue,' she declared after a moment's hesitation, 'but please don't think I'm unsympathetic. I dislike the idea of anyone being coerced into something they don't wish to do,' she ended defensively.

'Yes indeed, but I expect the Blanford woman would be the least concerned.'

'Is there nothing the police can do about it?'

He gave a mirthless laugh. 'As I said before, they have been unable to gather sufficient evidence. But before we go on, tell me what has changed—what causes you a problem more personal than that of your association with Meredith?'

Garland sighed. 'The trouble is, I'm worried that my sister may have got herself into a situation regarding her association with Meredith and her ex friend. It's nothing that I can put a name to, just a feeling that something awful will happen.' She shrugged, then continued, 'Really, I shouldn't have to worry about Sarah. She's nearly thirty, old enough to manage her own life.'

'I agree, you should not need to concern yourself,' said Nic, and as he spoke Garland became aware of his warm hands resting on her waist. The faintly caressing movement of his fingers awakening her senses as he drew her close to whisper against her hair, 'I do hope you have enjoyed this evening with me and you don't miss the glitzy night-life Meredith prefers.'

At the mere mention of Don her heart plummeted again. 'Oh please, Nic,' she entreated, 'it's not only concern for my sister, I want to put him from my mind even more.'

'Of course, forgive me,' he murmured, cupping her face in his hands.

Garland's spirits lifted once more as Nic's lips found hers, gently seeking a response. She experienced the same breathtaking sensation she'd had after dinner on that memorable first evening at Pedro's and her hands slid round his waist as the pressure of his lips increased.

*   *   *

Once back in the hotel she rang Sarah's number and still received no reply but, as she had stated earlier, Sarah was old enough to manage her own life. Even so, her concern had increased considerably and she decided, if she didn't get an answer the following morning, she would be obliged to ring Don however distasteful she found the thought of making contact with him. After what Nic had told her she had to warn Sarah and impress upon her that associating with Don and her ex friend, Patricia may mean she could be placing herself in an incriminating situation. Reflecting upon what she had heard her sister say over the phone only recently, when she had told someone they must do their own dirty work, Garland wondered if it had that been in connection with the matter Nic had now brought to her attention? Sarah had fairly regular appointments with her hairdresser at the salon she said Patricia had recommended. Could that mean her own sister had provided Patricia with an alibi?

It was as she undressed when she recalled having the telephone number of Sarah's ex fiancé, Mark Thomson, in her diary. Perhaps tomorrow, if she got no reply from Sarah she could try ringing Mark in case she'd decided to meet him somewhere.

But the following morning she was disappointed; no reply from the villa, and a very surprised response from Mark who had arrived at his place in southern France early the day before.

'Good to hear you, Garland! Yes, much to my delight Sarah telephoned me yesterday morning,' he told her.

'She hasn't arranged to meet you in France, has she? You see, I'm not at the villa at present, but I can't get a reply so I wondered if she was with you?'

'No, she's not here—wish she were—but I have promised to drive down to Spain once my work is completed on Sunday morning. Perhaps she's out shopping, she knows I'll be ravenous when I arrive, so there's no need for you to worry. I'll ring her myself before lunch.'

'Thanks, Mark, and if you manage to contact her before I do will you ask her to give me a call?'

Garland hadn't the heart to tell him she'd been trying to contact her sister since the previous afternoon. Now there was only one thing left to do. For her peace of mind she had to ring Don before she left for the course, and was relieved to find his number still listed in her diary.

The sleepy voice that responded to her call made her tremble with anger. She had a strong desire to challenge him about what Nic had told her but knew she must make an effort to be pleasant otherwise he may replace the receiver.

'Is Sarah with you?' she asked. 'I would like to speak to her, if I may . . .'

'Ah, Garland, it's you, darling!' he exclaimed, his voice brightening. 'Now, what's the problem?'

'I just want to speak to my sister, is she there?'

'Why don't we meet? You can speak to me instead.'

'No thanks, Don, I just want to contact Sarah. Did you see her last evening?'

'No, 'fraid not. Look, I'll send a car for you right away—we can chat . . .'

'I haven't time for that,' she broke in impatiently. 'Anyway, I'm not at the villa, so if you won't give me a direct answer I'll jolly well go to there and find her for myself!' With a sigh of exasperation she replaced the receiver.

As she prepared to go to breakfast with Simon she thought about her conversation with Nic the previous evening. What kind of employment had Don offered? He had wanted to know and she'd avoided giving an answer. But yes, soon after her arrival Don had suggested she could earn a considerable sum of money by delivering a vehicle of a more luxurious class to his business friend who lived in the south. In previous weeks he had employed Sarah, he'd told her, and stressed that she had been well rewarded for the job. Then he'd gone on to mention that the car was a left-hand drive and not difficult to manage, but being a little nervous of driving here until she'd had some practice Garland had declined which had been when her troubles began. And this reminded her, she hadn't noticed Sarah's large car in the garage during the past few days—rather a luxury, she'd thought—yet Sarah hadn't mentioned her intention to part with it.

* * *

'You seem rather preoccupied this morning,' Simon remarked after she joined him at his table. 'Did you manage to contact your sister?'

'No, that's what worries me. I even rang her

ex fiancé, Mark Thomson—you may have heard his name mentioned—he's got a place in France and tells me he will be driving down on Sunday.'

'Yes, I remember. Does that mean they've got together again?'

She shrugged. 'Hope so, he's such a nice guy. But now, before I go any further I'd like to know if I'm needed on the course this morning? I must admit I'm quite concerned about Sarah as she seemed upset when we last spoke and I haven't been able to reach her since.'

'Actually, you're not required to be there until the final day,' Simon said, 'though I'm sure you are worrying unnecessarily.'

'You may be right, but I prefer to see for myself. I'll be back this afternoon,' she promised. 'I won't be staying as I've got a dinner date at nine.'

'Of course, you're at liberty to come and go as you wish, but exactly what are you intending to do?'

'I'm going over to the villa, just to make sure she's all right. I wouldn't like to think she was ill, or had fallen, and no one was aware of it.'

'Have breakfast first,' he advised, 'then I'll run you to the station. But let me know if anything's wrong, and if you ring me to say what time you're coming back I can pick you up—or, depending on the time, maybe someone else would like to do the honours,' he added with a meaningful grin. 'You have my mobile number?'

'I think so, but I'll check.' Delving into her bag she withdrew her diary and opened it on the table. 'Yes, Simon it's here, and I also have your business card,' she told him slipping the printed card back into her bag.

'Now, eat your breakfast,' he said with a glint of humour in his eyes.

She smiled. 'Taking a rather paternal role, aren't you?'

'Don't want your father's wrath directed at me,' Simon grinned. 'He asked me to keep an eye on you.'

'Oh, he did, did he?' she said, and reaching over to the fruit bowl she rose from the table. 'Tell you what, I'll take an orange with me to keep you happy.'

'Better than nothing I suppose,' he said, taking his car keys from his pocket. 'Got everything you need?'

She nodded. But a short time later, as Simon maneuvered the hired car through the traffic, she realised she'd left her diary behind. 'I'm sure it was on the table, I must have put my napkin over it. Would you mind picking it up when you go back to the hotel?'

'Sure you won't need it?'

'No, I've got your card here, but I'd be grateful if you will hang on to it and I'll give you a call when I know the time of my train.'

'Good, I'll be there,' he said, shooting her a quick smile as he brought the car to a halt outside the station.

*   *   *

Just over an hour later Garland was walking briskly along the promenade in the direction of the villa. Deep in thought she almost missed seeing Pedro's raised hand as he hailed her from the café doorway.

'See you around midday,' she called and glanced up at the Tropic Hotel, thinking of Nic as she continued on her way. Member of staff indeed, she mused with shake of her head, she should have known.

Finding the door of the villa locked she took her key from her bag. Assuming Sarah was out on the patio at the other side of the house she called her name as she went through to the sitting room overlooking the garden. Seeing no sign of her there, or out on the patio, she went upstairs to search the bedrooms but her sister was nowhere to be found. Yet it appeared as though the daily help had been in that morning as everything was tidy and the beds made. Or was that yesterday, she wondered? Had Sarah slept here last night?

Hearing the slam of a car door, she thought it may be Sarah coming home, and crossing to the window she was in time to see two men alighting from a large car parked a little way along the road, a car she had noticed on her arrival. Now she saw the men advancing towards the house and turned to go downstairs as the knocker clattered on the heavy door.

She was half way down the stairs when the door opened and the two men stepped inside, their stance faintly intimidating as they waited for her to descend.

'Ah, *senorita* McLeod, at last!' said one with a triumphant leer as she reached the bottom step. 'The keys for the garage, if you please . . .'

'Certainly not!' she broke in defiantly, 'and what gives you the right to enter this house without being invited?'

'Police!' announced the older of the two men, and clicking his forefinger and thumb together demanded, 'Keys, *senorita*. Immediately!'

'I can't let you have any keys until you show me proof of your identity. I'm sure you appreciate my caution,' she said warily, then gave an involuntary gasp as she realised she had seen the older man before.

Ignoring her, the younger of the two pushed her aside to go towards the hall table where a bunch of keys lay beneath the mirror. Snatching them up he went outside, and soon after that there came the sound of a door crashing back on its hinges followed by an exclamation of fury.

'It is not here!' she understood the younger

man to say as he returned to the house. 'The car has gone!'

'I could have told you that! Perhaps now you will be good enough to leave' she said indignantly and attempted to usher them out. 'My sister will be furious when she hears about this!'

But both men stood their ground. 'Your sister?' queried the older man, his eyes narrowed.

'Yes, my sister . . .'

'Ah, your sister, now I understand,' he nodded, then demanded, 'Where she is now?'

'I don't know,' Garland snapped. 'I've been trying to contact her myself.'

'And the car?'

'I don't know that either . . .'

'The car,' he persisted, 'it is with your sister?'

'I haven't the faintest idea,' she said shortly, 'so I'd be grateful if you would leave. But if you like, I can leave her a message. Who shall I say called?'

'We will wait,' the older man said, hustling her towards the sitting room.

'Oh no, I want you to go, right now!' she cried, struggling against him, but immediately the younger man jumped to his aid and soon had her pinned to a chair in an inescapable grip.

'Now, you will please be quiet or Juan will gag you,' threatened the older of the two.

112

'That wouldn't be wise,' she retaliated. 'If I don't ring my colleague he's sure to telephone me here and he'll suspect something is wrong if there's no reply.'

'Of course,' said her captor with a smile, 'we must remedy that.' And he strolled over to where the telephone rested and yanked out the cable as he assured her smoothly, 'Now your colleague will not worry.' And crushing the connecting piece of plastic underfoot he addressed the younger man, Juan, when they exchanged a few swift words in their own language.

'I know you're not policemen!' she cried when he returned his attention to her, 'I've seen you somewhere quite recently, and if you don't leave this house I shall call for help.' With that, she opened her mouth to let out an ear-piercing scream.

'*Dios!*' cried Juan, releasing one of her wrists to clap his hand over her mouth. But he quickly snatched it away when she sank her teeth into the flesh of his index finger.

'*Cannibal!*' she heard him shriek and ducked to avoid his raised hand. But the other man stepped sharply forward to intervene, saying he wanted no violence toward the *senorita*, and produced a navy blue patterned scarf which she recognised as being like one belonging to Patricia. Giving her a warning wag of his finger he tossed it over to Juan, instructing him to place it over her mouth

113

should she make another sound.

'You understand?' he said. 'He releases you if you stay in the chair, yes?'

Suddenly convinced that both these men were those she had seen with Patricia in the restaurant the evening before Garland strove to collect her wits. Aware they had the upper hand she nodded and searched her mind for another solution to her predicament. It was useless screaming to attract attention—the villa stood well apart from other dwellings— she would have to think of a scheme to distract them. 'No violence,' the older man—who Juan addressed as *senor* Gomez—had said which must mean she was of greater value to him if she were unharmed. But if she inflicted an injury upon herself, or became ill for some reason, would they panic and abandon the idea of keeping her prisoner here?

Senor Gomez made himself comfortable in an easy chair while Juan fixed his attention on the road outside. And the tension within her mounted as she struggled to think of a means of escape until a sudden flash of inspiration had her moaning softly and holding her head in her hands.

Immediately, Juan sprang forward but the older man put out a restraining hand to prevent him reaching her. '*Senorita*, what is wrong?' he asked, his hand tilting her chin to observe her more closely. 'Why do you make this noise?'

She shook her head and said in a weak voice, 'It's nothing, just the usual . . .'

'The usual—what is this?'

'It's a while since I've eaten anything, but if I just take a little sugar . . .'

'Take a little sugar?' he echoed. 'Why is this?'

'I'm diabetic, but if I have some sugar I should be all right.'

She understood him to repeat what she had said to the younger man as he nodded in the direction of the kitchen.

'It's all right, I have some with me,' she said, pointing to her bag.

Retrieving the bag, he gave her a twisted smile. 'No tricks,' he said, 'no mobile telephone,' and instead of handing it to her he emptied its contents on the coffee table before inviting her to take what she needed.

Spotting the sugar packet she'd picked up in Pedro's café she opened it carefully at one end and tipped half the contents into her mouth. Reaching for her pen she explained, 'I must now make a note of the time otherwise I may forget when I have to prepare for my next injection.' And shaking the sugar to one end of the packet, she wrote the time as clearly as space would allow then, appearing to doodle, she drew circles in the shape of a snail before sliding the little packet back on the table.

Appearing a little uneasy, Gomez said, 'So, to avoid further problems it is better you tell me what time your sister arrives, otherwise you come with us.'

'Where exactly do you intend taking me?' she asked and he laughed and turned to the younger man to repeat her question.

Juan also seemed to find this amusing and responded in his own tongue when a word sounding like Meredith came into the rapid conversation, followed by another word she recognised, *Escudellers,* the name of the street where the restaurant called 'The Snails' was situated.

'Do not worry, you will receive medical attention there,' Gomez informed her, 'but if your sister is arriving soon we shall have the information we need.'

'But I've already told you, I have no idea when she will be back . . .'

'We will wait one half hour more, after that you will leave for her a message. You will ask her to drive to your hotel in the city—tell her it is very urgent.'

'Why should I?' she persisted and saw him raise his eyes to the ceiling.

The next thirty minutes seemed like an eternity to Garland. During this time Juan had hardly taken his eyes off her, while the older man spent his time glancing through pages of advertisements for cars in a glossy English magazine.

Glancing at his watch, Gomez rose and came to stand in front of her. *'Senorita,* you will leave for your sister a message. Immediately!' he stressed, seeing her defiant expression.

Reaching for Simon's card which lay on the table amongst the contents of her bag, she told him coolly, 'The name of my hotel is on here so I'll write a note on the back and leave it for her to see.'

As she wrote he looked on, nodding when the brief message was completed. But once he glanced away to speak to Juan she drew another quick imitation of a snail along with a question mark on the reverse of the card and placed it on the table near to the half empty packet of sugar. Then, under his watchful eye she returned the rest of her belongings to her bag before Juan hurried her out to their quite luxurious car with its sumptuous upholstery and darkened windows.

Seated in the back with *senor* Gomez beside her and Juan in the driving seat, she heard the click of the automatic door locks. Desperate to escape, she ran her fingers across her forehead and gasped for air; they would soon be passing Pedro's place and as she was seated on the side nearest to the café she hoped to give Pedro a signal.

'Can you open the window?' she pleaded. 'I feel faint—I need some air.'

'Juan, the air conditioning!' Gomez demanded and immediately she heard the faint hum in response when he turned to her to enquire, 'It is better now?'

'I would much prefer the window open. It is so claustrophobic in here.'

'But this car has every comfort,' he said, sounding surprised to hear her criticism. 'It is similar to the one your sister drives, yes?'

'I don't understand you—my sister doesn't have a car now . . .'

'She has sold it, maybe?'

'She doesn't own a car, of this class or any other,' she persisted bravely, though inwardly she trembled.

'So, she has taken the car to another person, yes?'

'Look here, I have no idea what type of car my sister may have driven, so why do you keep asking me these ridiculous questions?'

She heard him utter a hiss of impatience, and as they sped past Pedro's place she lost all hope of attracting anyone's attention to her plight. What was the connection between these men and the car Sarah once had, she wondered as they left the little town behind to take the main road to the city? Also, she was sure she'd heard the word Meredith spoken during conversation between her captors, and as a vehicle seemed to be the main reason for their visit, was its existence in any way connected with Don? She drew a sudden breath, reflecting upon the employment Don had offered, employment she had felt bound to reject, but which had incited his unreasonable fury.

Deep in thought, her eyes downcast for most of the journey, she was suddenly aware the car was drawing to a halt. Raising her head, she saw they had pulled up in a very narrow street with old buildings towering darkly on either side in what she assumed to be the old quarter of the city. Then the door locks were released and, aided by Juan, Gomez took her arm in a firm grip to pull her out of the car and in through the doorway of the nearest building.

The entrance to the old building was dimly lit and uninviting. And once the door had been locked behind them Gomez ushered her along the passage towards a flight of stone steps where a small lamp hung from the high, beamed ceiling. Indicating she should go up ahead, he nodded towards the left-hand door at the top where she hesitated, wondering what lay ahead.

'Please, *senorita*, enter,' he instructed, nudging her forward. 'You will stay here while we wait for your sister.'

Terrified, she tried to turn away, but he was too strong for her and she felt herself being thrust forward into a large, well-furnished hall. After the dim exterior this was quite unexpected, and her eyes widened in surprise as she took in the subdued wall lights shining across an ornate gilt framed mirror.

Shrugging off her captor, she gasped, 'Why

have you brought me here?'

'To discover exactly what little game your sister is playing,' came a voice from a doorway at the far side of the hall, a voice she immediately recognised.

'Don!' she cried going to confront him. 'How dare you trick me like this? I thought I'd made it quite clear, I didn't want to see you ever again . . .'

'Quiet, woman!' he snarled, and reaching out he yanked her into the spacious sitting room behind him where, reclining on a huge settee, she saw the smiling figure of Patricia Blanford.

CHAPTER SEVEN

The shock of seeing Patricia rendered Garland speechless. Then, from somewhere behind, she heard Gomez speak in English, reminding her that Don spoke little of the local language. 'This is the sister,' she heard him explain.

'I know that you fool!' Don snapped. 'I told you to get them both here.'

'The other one is not there,' replied Gomez, flushed with indignation. 'We are waiting—she does not come to the villa—we leave instructions for her. Also, this one is ill . . . diabetic, she says.'

'First I've heard of it! Now, let's get back to

more urgent matters,' Don demanded. 'The vehicle? Any trace of that?'

Garland felt impelled to intervene and quickly found her voice. 'There has not been a car at the villa since soon after I arrived . . .'

Don turned to her and snarled, 'You keep your mouth shut!'

'I will not!' she retaliated, her heart beating wildly. 'And if you intend to make trouble for my sister you'll hear about it!'

'Oh yea, from whom?' he challenged, shooting her a disdainful glance.

'From my father, that's who!'

'Your father? After what Sarah told me, I expect he'll be glad to be rid of her,' he gloated, and turning to Patricia demanded, 'Can't you do something useful and keep this creature quiet?'

'Oh dear, we are in a mood today,' Patricia remarked acidly as she rose from the settee. 'What do you expect me to do, gag her?'

'You don't frighten me!' Garland declared as the strikingly beautiful woman strolled towards her. 'In fact, once the authorities hear of this it will be exactly the opposite!'

'Hear that, Don, she's threatening me,' Patricia sneered. 'She's braver than her stupid sister.'

'Sarah is not stupid!' Garland cried. 'Unless you consider her stupid because she wasn't willing to become involved in your illegal racket. But I believe you're quite experienced in the motor trade, Patricia. Am I correct?' she asked pointedly and saw the woman's quick glance in Don's direction when she had the satisfaction of knowing she'd hit the mark.

Don gave a twisted smile as he turned to the woman. 'You see,' he said, 'I warned you that so called friend of yours wasn't to be trusted. After all her whining about wanting the good life, she hadn't the guts to give it a go.'

'If you are referring to my sister,' Garland burst in, 'let me assure you she was not the one to inform me about your racket . . .'

'But if it wasn't Sarah, then I'd like to know who else has been telling you tales,' Patricia interjected, her eyes narrowed.

'Yes, I'm sure you would,' retorted Garland with a lift of her chin. 'But I don't intend staying here until you find out!'

'You were offered the same perks but you were too scared to take it on, otherwise you wouldn't be here,' Don sneered. 'But I intend you shall stay until your sister decides to make an appearance so I suggest you shut it!' Directing his attention to the older man he glanced at his watch and said, 'Give it half an hour, then you'd better check if the other one has turned up at the hotel. You know what she looks like—red hair, tall . . .'

Garland began to edge her way towards the door, hoping to make a dash for it when Gomez left, but Juan spotted her movement and barred her way.

'I'm finding you increasingly difficult to tolerate,' said Don, and on a signal from him Juan hustled her through the sitting room and out onto a wide balcony, locking the door behind her.

She realized she was at the rear of the building and now the sun had moved off the balcony, exposing her to the cool April air. Going across to the railing she leant over in the hope of spotting a way down, but even from this first floor, the height from the ground made leaving by this route impossible.

With a heavy heart she went to perch on the edge of one of the reclining chairs, her mind centered on a means of escape. Her thoughtful gaze followed a wasp as it buzzed round a pot of scarlet geraniums. Envying its freedom, she wondered what Simon's reaction would be when she didn't telephone him as promised? And if she didn't contact him, knowing she had made arrangements for dinner later that evening, would he think to mention it to Nic? She just had to find a solution as the longer she was kept prisoner here, the greater the chance of Sarah being found at the hotel and brought to join her—assuming Sarah was sufficiently concerned to co-operate with her request.

*   *   *

As Garland strove to suppress her fear of what

123

was in store for her, she was unaware of the anxiety Simon was suffering as he slid his mobile phone into his pocket and hurried back to the clubhouse. There, he went to the payphone and keyed in the number of the villa, but again he got the strange tone, which sounded as though the number was not available.

Uttering a sigh of frustration he went back on the course, ensuring his mobile was switched on as he made his way to the seventeenth green. He had already made the decision, once play was over there was nothing to prevent him taking a ride to the villa to make sure everything was all right. Garland had a reputation of being someone who could be relied upon, yet her lack of communication was puzzling and he was beginning to worry. James McLeod would expect him to show concern for his daughter so a check on her whereabouts would be sure to meet with his approval.

Waiting for the final players to come in, Simon spotted Nic amongst the spectators on the eighteenth green. Nic had played another brilliant round and appeared relaxed as he watched the last player's final shot. Simon wondered if he had received a call from Garland and, although he didn't want to worry Nic, an enquiry may mean his journey would not be necessary.

'Hi, Nic, good game today, heh?' he said

cheerfully as the star player advanced toward him.

'Yes, but it was stiff competition. The course is in marvelous condition,' Nic commented then, glancing beyond Simon, asked, 'Garland not with you?'

'No she's not, which is why I'd like to know if she has been in contact with you today?'

'Today, no. However, I expect to see her this evening.' Nic paused as he caught sight of the other man's anxious expression. 'You look worried, my friend, is something wrong?'

Simon began to explain the reason Garland had gone to the villa, adding the fact she had not telephoned him as promised. 'And I've tried the clubhouse phone,' he added, 'but the line seems to be dead.'

'Maybe her sister is away today,' Nic suggested. 'If you are acquainted with her, you will know she is not the kind of person to sit in the house all day.'

'No, we've never met, but I'm rather concerned because of what happened yesterday when Garland rang her. She told me Sarah had sounded distressed, seemed almost frightened. In fact, she described Sarah as being a bit hysterical and had spoken of her intention to contact her ex-fiancé.'

'Maybe Sarah is with the fiancé . . .' Nic started to say but Simon raised a hand to interrupt him as he pulled Garland's diary from his pocket.

'You could be right, and I'm sure she'll have his number somewhere in here,' he said. 'Ah yes, here it is—Mark Thomson—he's on business in France. I'll give him a bell.'

But when Simon got the required number he groaned. 'It's someone speaking in French—not my best subject—are you familiar with the language?'

Nic smiled and took the handpiece from Simon when he sounded as fluent in that language as he was in English. 'It is the concierge, he tells me that Mr. Thomson is attending a conference today,' he translated for Simon's benefit, then continued, 'No, he's not had a visitor, nor any message regarding a Miss Sarah McLeod. But Mr. Thomson is leaving for Spain on Sunday morning.'

'Oh, I see. So now we don't seem able to locate either Garland or Sarah,' said Simon, dispiritedly. 'Perhaps I'd better take a ride over to the villa to check for any sign of them there.'

'I'll come with you,' was Nic's immediate response, 'and if you have no objection we will go in my car as I am more familiar with the road.'

Simon's features brightened. 'Thanks, in any case, your car is sure to be faster than the one I've hired.'

*   *   *

Alone on the balcony, looking down on the narrow city street, Garland shivered. The tall buildings opposite kept off the sunlight and the chilling breeze made her position extremely cheerless and uncomfortable. She had been determined not to beg to be allowed indoors, but now she was beginning to consider her rather stubborn decision as merely fanciful heroics.

She worried about Sarah, wondering if the instruction to come to the hotel would land her sister in this same situation. She considered offering to strike a bargain with Don by accepting the employment he had previously been so insistent she take in exchange for her own and Sarah's release.

Finally, she tried appealing to Patricia when she made one of her regular appearances at the window. But it was hopeless, she had merely pulled the curtain aside to send her a gloating smile before letting it fall back into place. Who could help her out of this quandary, she wondered desperately; would Simon raise the alarm when she didn't telephone? Would he contact her father, or the police, once he realised she wasn't returning to the hotel? And with too much time to think she began to fret over what Nic's reaction would be when she didn't appear in the foyer of the hotel as arranged. Would he be very upset not to find her there, or did he consider her merely a transient distraction from the stress of his professional life? Her throat ached from unshed tears as she fought against the thought. Closing her eyes, she pictured his smile and recalled the tender moments they had spent together, convincing herself that Nic cared.

*   *   *

Nic certainly knew the road to the villa and they covered it at speed, arriving well before the time Simon had anticipated. Hurrying from the car he went to lift the iron knocker, only realising the heavy door was unlocked when it swung open beneath his hand and he stumbled into the dim, cool hall.

Observing this from his position in the driver's seat, Nic quickly alighted and went to join him, but there was total silence in response to their calls. And when Nic ventured into the large sunlit lounge he saw no sign of anyone there, or out on the patio, so both he and Simon decided to investigate the villa's upper floor.

'Strange, no-one is here, particularly as the place is open,' said Nic as he wandered back to the sitting room. 'You've checked both bathrooms?' he queried when Simon joined him.

'Yes, Nic. I didn't like going in but there's no sign of her anywhere.'

'Mm, like you, I feel as if I'm intruding,' said

Nic thoughtfully as he paced the room. 'But also like you, I'm worried,' he added, returning to where Simon was standing when his gaze fell on the long coffee table, his attention caught by the familiar design on a packet of sugar beside a business card which, on closer inspection, he found to be one of Simon's.

'Simon! Here, take a look,' he instructed. 'You see, it is a message for Sarah asking her to go to your hotel.'

'Yes, it's Garland's handwriting, and there's the orange she took with her so at least we know she's been here. But why didn't she ring to say she was leaving? I've had my mobile switched on all day—it's very worrying . . .' He paused, hearing Nic's soft curse as he lifted the receiver of the telephone which stood on the table.

'The line is dead,' Nic declared, frowning, and tracing the cable over to the wall he saw it had been wrenched from the socket and the plastic connector lay in pieces on the floor beneath it.

'It must have happened before Garland arrived or she would have rung me, I know,' Simon decided. 'And she must have known her sister wouldn't be back until much later, otherwise she would have waited instead of writing this message on my card.'

'Yes indeed,' said Nic, scrutinising the message. 'It also means it happened after Garland rang here last night. She got no reply, but the line was not dead.'

Simon shook his head. 'Or this morning, there was no answer but she didn't say anything about the line being dead. Yet, if no one was here, who could have disconnected the phone, and why?'

'Exactly, so it must have been cut off sometime between her leaving the hotel and arriving here,' Nic decided. 'And, as she couldn't contact you from here she would either go to the nearest call box, or head straight back to the city.'

'I hope you're right, Nic, but I would have thought she'd have left the place secure, wouldn't you?'

Nic nodded. 'We can check the nearby telephone boxes as we leave, and I will enquire at Pedro's on our way. She may have called there as I see one of his little sugar packets on the table.'

'We had better leave the message where it was in case Sarah gets back,' said Simon, 'but I still can't understand why Garland wants her sister to join us at the hotel—it's most peculiar.'

Nic wrinkled his nose and turned the business card over to study it again. Pointing to a scribble on the side of the card bearing Simon's name he asked, 'What do you make of that—was it there when you gave it to her?'

Taking the card, Simon shook his head. 'Looks like she's been doodling,' he suggested with a short laugh as he returned it to the table.

Nic glanced up. 'Doodling . . .?' he queried thoughtfully. 'To me, it looks more like she was trying to draw a snail.'

'Hey, look, it's also on the sugar packet! Also the numbers one, a dot, and fifteen. Do you think she could have been writing the time?'

Nic frowned. 'If she wrote it today it would be thirteen fifteen, no?'

'Not the way she would write it. You forget, we don't generally use a twenty-four hour clock.'

Nic clicked his tongue as he compared the figures on the little packet. 'Yes, you're right, I should have known. And this doodle, as you call it, also looks like a snail . . .' He gave a gentle shake of his head and murmured, 'Snail, one fifteen, and a question mark . . . I wonder if it is a message of some sort?'

Confident Sarah would be returning that day, they closed the doors and left the villa. Driving down to the quiet little town, Nic pulled over to Pedro's café and alighted, concealing a rather anxious smile over his brief reminiscence of an evening he had shared with Garland. But in minutes he was back in the driving seat, spreading his hands in a desultory fashion as he related to Simon, 'She told Pedro she would call on her way back to the station, around mid-day. However, he has not seen her since she passed by this morning which makes me wonder if there is a connection with the time on the packet. Also, the more I think about it, why draw a snail?'

'A snail . . .' Simon repeated, glancing across at Nic. 'Yes, if that's what it is, why on earth would she do that?'

'It could be a clue as it was something we joked about. Even so, she wouldn't expect me to be at the villa to see it.'

Simon knitted his brows. 'A clue to what?'

'Your hotel is quite close to *Los Caracoles*, the restaurant Garland and I visited last night,' Nic explained. 'And it was there that we spotted a woman who is, or was, acquainted with Garland's sister—a woman possessing a rather dubious reputation.'

'I think you had better tell me about her,' Simon said.

*   *   *

Garland looked up to see the darkening sky and her shivering increased. She had considered dropping the ceramic pot containing the geranium down to the street below with the hope of attracting attention, but during the time she had been on the balcony the area below was always deserted and the windowless building opposite looked like a warehouse. She felt certain she was going to be held here overnight and had come to the conclusion the only way to placate Don was to apologise and agree to take the employment he had offered. The next time Patricia came to the window she would beg to be allowed in.

But it was Don who came to unlock the door. 'You can come inside now,' he said with a jerk of his head to indicate she should enter, 'but for God's sake behave yourself and keep quiet.'

'Yes, Don, and I'm sorry I said all those things to you,' she said, her tone submissive as they entered the house. 'You see, I was just a bit worried about Sarah . . . is she here yet?'

'No she is not,' he spat out, 'but you'll damned well stay here until she is!'

'Can we not come to some arrangement—about employment I mean—can we discuss it? I must admit I could do with the money—Sarah must have been mad to give it up—and I wouldn't mention it to anyone if that's how you want it . . .'

'My God, you've changed your tune! Well, you can forget it—she was too well known and I wouldn't trust either of you, not now. People don't mess with me a second time and get away with it!'

Garland's heart sank but she didn't give up. 'Look, Don, I was new here, but now I've got used to the place and I've had time to think about it . . .'

'Yes, I'm sure you have, but you can stop

your nagging, woman, it doesn't cut any ice with me.'

'But surely you don't intend to keep me here? My colleague will . . .'

'Never mind your colleague, it's your father you should worry about,' he said, his beady eyes narrowing as he added, 'Yes, it will be very interesting to see how highly James McLeod values his daughters!'

For a moment Garland didn't catch Don's meaning, but a glance at his smug expression soon made clear his intention. 'If you think my father will fall for that you are very much mistaken. He wouldn't listen to threats from anyone, you least of all.'

Don merely raised his eyebrows. 'We will see,' he said, then went on to add, 'Any moment now Patricia will be bringing your dinner—can't have you complaining to McLeod about your treatment—but I'll be dining at my club. Must attend to business, you know, so when Patricia and the boy return I'm off.'

'Do you mean Juan? I thought both he and the other man had gone to meet my sister?'

Don chuckled. 'Don't you worry, Gomez has a way with the ladies. He can be extremely charming when he chooses so he won't need Juan's assistance. Oh yes, if necessary he can be very persuasive so he'll have no problems with Sarah.'

'Then he's certainly taking his time!' she

134

shot back. 'I'd be a bit worried about him if I were you.'

'Well, if she doesn't turn up, I'm sure just one of you will be enough to persuade Daddy to part with his cash,' he jeered. 'And you must admit, if Sarah has read your message she's in no particular hurry to see you!'

*   *   *

Simon blew out his cheeks. 'This Blanford woman sounds a bit dodgy to me,' he said when Nic had finished speaking. 'Hardly the sort of person Garland would associate with, but I can't speak for Sarah as we've never actually met.'

Nic nodded. 'Garland did not seem endeared towards her, and she told me her sister had ceased to be associated with Blanford a few days ago. But, before that, it is my belief both these women were driving for Meredith.'

'This steal to order is quite a racket, I believe,' said Simon. 'Usually the luxury class of car, or Four by Four's, anything pricey. Amazes me how they get into them in the first instance, the owners always swear they were locked, and in some cases alarmed as well.'

'And someone has to drive them down from the ferries,' Nic pointed out. Has Garland ever mentioned the sort of work Meredith offered her, or has she told you what her sister does for a living?'

'By what she said the other morning, I understand Sarah was an actress until a few months ago, then it seems she had a disagreement with her father and came here to live. Had the chance of a lift with this Blanford woman, so my boss tells me, though he never really trusted her and thought she was a bad influence on Sarah.'

Nic compressed his lips and concentrated on his driving until they came to a sign for the airport where he turned off and drew the car to a halt.

'Garland wouldn't fly home without telling me, if that's what you're thinking,' Simon said quickly and insisted, 'I just know she wouldn't let me down.'

'Or me, I hope,' Nic murmured, then continued, 'Earlier you told me Garland had the impression her sister seemed nervous, or even frightened, so perhaps we should take a look round the departure area in case Sarah decided to go home.'

'You mean Garland could be seeing her off?' Simon gave a snort of laughter. 'How ironic,' he said. 'Her only reason for coming here was to persuade Sarah to go home, and now you're suggesting it could be the other way round.'

Nic shook his head. 'We don't know that yet, but we have to start looking somewhere. Try ringing the hotel again in case she's gone back there.'

After a few minutes Simon reported that she wasn't in the hotel. 'So if she's not at the airport what the devil will we do next?' he asked worriedly. 'Perhaps I should let her father know.'

'First we will check the airport,' Nic decided as he drove off. 'If she's not there, or back at the hotel, we will pay another visit to the villa.'

'So I'll not ring my boss just yet as I don't want to alarm him,' said Simon, 'although I'm beginning to get very worried myself.'

In the busy airport they searched the departure area and the airport railway station in case she was taking a train back to the city. But there was no sign of Garland or her sister, and the last flight to her home destination had been gone for almost an hour.

'Back to the villa,' said Nic as they returned to his car. 'And, if there is no-one there, we telephone the hotel again as she will have had ample time to reach it by then.'

The villa was as silent as when they had left it, and the hotel reported her key was still in the slot and had been since she had left for the station with Simon that morning. Disappointed by the fruitless journey they agreed it was now time to inform the police, until Nic suggested they check again with Pedro before going any further.

Seated at a table on the patio they sipped the coffee Pedro had insisted on serving. And

137

the restaurant owner's face creased with concern when told the reason for their visit.

'Are you sure she did not call here after one-fifteen?' Nic asked him. 'She had written that time on one of your little sugar packets,' he continued, indicating the similar item in his saucer. 'Did she pick up one of these today?'

'No, the *senorita* never arrives,' Pedro replied worriedly. 'She did not take the sugar today.'

Nic had emptied one sugar packet into his coffee, and taking a pen from his pocket he wrote one-fifteen the way Garland had then scribbled the same circular design beside it.

'Yes, that's just the way she drew it,' Simon observed, 'and the same thing on the card, plus the question mark.'

'Ah, *caracoles!*' exclaimed Pedro. 'Maybe she is liking the snails . . .'

'Snails . . .' Nic repeated thoughtfully and thrust a note at Pedro as he rose hurriedly from the table. 'For the coffee,' he said. 'Come, Simon, back to the city, those snails she drew have given me an idea.'

CHAPTER EIGHT

To avoid a further altercation with Don, Garland lay back in an easy chair at the far end of the sitting room and feigned sleep.

Raising her eyelids a fraction she saw him cast an impatient glance at his watch as he moved restlessly round the room, and wondered if Sarah had arrived at the hotel, or had her sister chosen to ignore the message she'd left on Simon's business card?

The sound of Patricia's voice along with the tap of her high heels on the tiled hall floor interrupted her troubled thoughts. 'Food for the prisoner!' she heard the woman announce as she peered into the sitting room. 'Hey, it looks as though madam's asleep—I could have saved my money!'

'Don't be so damned glib,' Don admonished, his voice fading a little as he followed her into the kitchen to continue, 'We don't want an ailing hostage, so let's not have any more cracks like that!'

'Well I hope you don't think I'm going to act as her servant . . .'

'Keep your voice down, woman. Another twenty-four hours and we'll be laughing,' said Don confidently. 'McLeod won't object to handing over the cash once he's at the villa and sees evidence of his dear Sarah's misdeeds.'

'Thank God you discovered the location of the er . . . evidence as you call it,' said Patricia. 'But I can't understand what made her dump it there—the silly bitch would have been well paid if she'd done as you asked.'

Don put a finger to his lips and lowered his

voice, 'She informed our man at the garage it had broken down but, fortunately, she said where it was so he rang me. He'd been told to expect another Four by Four but thought he'd better check. I've asked him to leave it where it is, we'll pick it up after dark.'

'Do you want me to drive it to the villa when it has been fixed?'

Garland had to strain her ears to catch Don's next words. 'Yes, and take Juan with you. I'll ring the garage and get him to sort out any fault.'

'With the original plates?' asked Patricia in hushed tones.

Don merely chuckled and replied softly, 'Why not? No point in changing anything until McLeod has seen proof of his daughter's criminal activities. Afterwards, I'll have a word with our friend about making the necessary alterations. I've got the paperwork ready, and a set of VIN plates ready.'

'VIN plates—what are they?'

'They're vehicle identification number plates of course, just waiting to be bolted on, so don't you worry, darling. This will be better than our hostage plan which would only draw sympathy, whereas this way his good name's at stake so whichever way things turn out we'll not be the losers.'

'Brilliant, Don, you've thought of everything,' Patricia praised him. 'Now, I'd better wake her up and get the food out of the microwave. Then, once Gomez gets back, Juan and I can go and move that vehicle. By the way, he's been gone for ages, do you think Juan should go and check what's happening?'

*   *   *

'Where exactly are we going?' Simon asked as they moved in and out of the lines of traffic in the busy city streets.

As they waited at the traffic lights Nic shot him a sideways glance and said, 'There was something about the snail Garland drew that made me wonder if by chance it was a clue. I think I told you, last evening we had dinner at the restaurant, *Los Caracoles*, and that was where we saw the Blanford woman buying food to take out, presumably to eat at home, or wherever she is living.'

'And you suspect this woman is connected with Garland's disappearance?'

Nic nodded. 'It is quite possible. Two men accompanied her, though what the connection is I do not know, but I thought another visit might give us an opportunity to see her again. Perhaps she's known there—the staff may help.'

*   *   *

When Garland sensed movement nearby she pretended to rouse from sleep, yawning and stretching so as not to awaken any suspicion Don and Patricia may have about her overhearing their conversation. It was becoming very clear that vehicles of some kind played a key part in both their lives and were somehow connected with Sarah's problems.

'What time is it?' she asked, catching Don's attention as she squinted sleepily at her watch. 'Sarah isn't here, is she?'

'Don't you worry, she soon will be,' he said, yet she sensed uncertainty in his tone as he glanced at his watch yet again.

'Perhaps you were right, Don, she's in no great hurry to see me. She may not even bother so there is no point in you keeping me here.'

'I shall decide when you leave, until then I suggest you eat your meal,' he said, indicating for her to move to the dining area next to the kitchen.

'And will the lady take wine with her meal?' Patricia sneered as she beckoned Garland to follow.

'Of course,' said Garland, 'providing it hasn't been acquired illegally.'

'You think you're clever, don't you,' Patricia bridled, 'but you'll soon regret it when Don's had a word with your father.'

Inwardly distressed by her situation, but determined not to show it, Garland merely shrugged. Taking the dish from the microwave, she seated herself at the table and lifted the lid, releasing the cloud of steam rising from the portion of roasted chicken within. On the table, contained in a cornucopia made of paper, she discovered a bread roll that was baked in the shape of a snail. At the sight of the bread her heart jolted and she felt a stab of emotion, remembering the previous evening when she had dined at *Los Caracoles* with Nic, and where they had seen Patricia purchase food. Had this meal come from the same restaurant? If so, this meant it would be in the locality of her hotel. But, even if Simon should discover his business card at the villa, it was unlikely he would connect the restaurant with the snail she had hastily scribbled upon it. If only Nic could see it, she thought with a soft groan, he would recall seeing Patricia there and may realise it was a clue. But then, what use would that be, she asked herself as a tear escaped to run down her cheek. Unless she could attract someone's attention to her predicament, such a clue was of no help whatsoever.

*   *   *

'No sign of her in the hotel, Nic,' Simon announced as he came back through the reception area. 'What do you suggest we do next?'

Pretending interest in the posters advertising local events, Nic beckoned him

143

into the foyer to ask, 'Did you see the man who left as we came in?'

'Yes, do you know him?' Simon queried. 'I noticed him standing outside when we arrived, before we went to park the car.'

'He's nowhere in sight now but he seemed familiar. When you went to your room I thought I overheard him asking for someone, and I'm certain the receptionist told him *senorita* McLeod had not been back since this morning.'

'Ah, but was he asking for Garland or Sarah?'

'*Senorita* McLeod could have meant either of them, I agree, but as Garland left a message for Sarah to come here it must mean neither have arrived.'

Simon looked anxious. 'I think it's time I rang the boss, don't you?'

'In a moment, after we have called in the restaurant where I saw the Blanford woman last night. And the man we saw leave the hotel—I said he looked familiar—well I'm convinced he was one of the men with her.'

In the restaurant Nic made for the table he had shared with Garland the previous evening, and indicated the area below. 'There, Simon, by the cash desk, we saw her and the man who just left the hotel, the other was younger.'

'Do you suppose that indicates they live somewhere in this part of town?'

Nic nodded. 'The Blanford women

144

appeared to know the two men, but if she is staying with them, or she has a place of her own, I'm not sure, yet I wouldn't expect anyone to purchase food here if they didn't live nearby.'

'What about that chap Garland knew—Meredith, I believe his name was—any idea where he hangs out?'

'He owns a nightclub in the city, but I'm not sure if he lives on the premises,' Nic said, reaching for the menu. 'Now, let's eat, you must be starving.'

Simon looked doubtful, but Nic insisted when he realised it would be around the same time as he and Garland had dined here the evening before.

After a hurried meal they lingered over coffee, their tension increasing when neither the Blanford woman, nor her companions, put in an appearance.

Downstairs again, at the cash desk, Nic hung back until the other customers dispersed. Withdrawing some notes from his wallet he enquired of the cashier, 'I had hoped to meet a relative of mine, but I must have missed her. I believe she was here last night—comes to buy dinner for herself and her friends.'

Simon saw the cashier frown as he checked the bill and handed Nic his change. It looked as though they were out of luck until he heard Nic continue, 'I'm sure you will know her, she's slim, quite tall . . . has long auburn hair . . .

well, shoulder length,' he corrected with a gesture of his hand.

The cashier gave a shrug, appearing to show little interest. Nic pocketed his change and withdrew another note from the wallet when the man asked suddenly. 'She is English? Usually with a gentleman—sometimes two?'

'Yes, yes, you are right. I knew you would recognise her.'

'It is the red hair,' he said. 'She was here this evening, buys more food today. Maybe she has guests . . .'

'Ah no, I have missed her!' Nic broke in with a groan, yet inwardly his hopes were rising. And he uttered a long sigh as he continued his lie, 'She has moved to another apartment since we last met, but perhaps you can tell me where she now lives. You may know her number, it will not be far from here.'

The cashier shrugged again. 'I am sorry *senor*, I can not tell you which is the building but I know it is in this street because sometimes she is back very quickly—only moments—if she has visitors, or needs extra bread.'

Nic thanked him, pressing the note into the man's hand as he said, 'For the service, *senor*. This is an excellent restaurant, we have enjoyed our meal.'

'I could follow most of that,' said Simon as they left the restaurant, 'but we still don't know where Garland is. Do you think it possible she and Sarah have gone out for the day and we are worrying unnecessarily?'

'No, I don't think so. You said yourself it would be uncharacteristic of her to change her plans without letting you know. In addition to that, don't forget the telephone had been wrenched out, the door was unlocked, and she did not appear at Pedro's after telling him she would call.'

Simon nodded. 'Yes, you're right, so what do we do next?'

'Perhaps it would be wise to get some advice before we do anything further,' Nic said, his expression grave. 'I can't bear the suspense, worrying about what has happened to Garland, but I know just the man to ask.'

'Anything that will clear up this mystery, you can count me in,' Simon agreed. 'It seems to me you're as concerned as I am, and it's my guess you like her just a bit more than you'll admit.'

Nic cast him a sideways glance and nodded. 'Like her?' he said softly. 'I would not have believed it possible to feel so much affection for anyone in such a short time, but now I do.'

*   *   *

Don's patience was getting shorter and his temper growing worse. Garland thought it wiser to remain in the dining room until he calmed down.

147

'Where the devil have you been, Gomez?' she heard him snarl. 'I told you not to come back without her.'

'I think she is not coming,' she heard the man respond. 'I have been waiting for many hours, I am tired of this . . .'

'You won't be complaining when you have the cash in your hand, will you?' Don grated. 'Your sort never do!'

'This was not the deal we made!' Gomez retaliated furiously. 'It is not my fault she is not arriving . . .'

'Hey, you'll gain nothing by arguing,' Patricia intervened. 'Anyway, what's the problem? Let McLeod think they're both here—he's not to know.'

'Do you imagine I hadn't already thought of that?' Don sneered, 'The car's a bonus!' Turning to address Gomez, he directed, 'Take another look, if there's nothing doing then we'll give McLeod a bell.'

'I look one more time, no more,' Gomez declared firmly, 'then I bring more food from the restaurant—Juan has eaten everything that was left.' He hesitated as something occurred to him, then said, 'I hope you remember, the *senorita* is diabetic,' before going on to relate what happened at the villa.

'Diabetic! It's the first I've heard of it,' Patricia said, and Don frowned.

To Garland he snarled, 'Now, I think you'd better tell me, exactly what little game you're playing?'

*   *   *

'At least we know Sarah is safe,' said Nic, pausing on the pavement of the busy narrow street as he returned his mobile to his pocket. 'And the vehicle and garage are under surveillance. The officer has been trying to contact me at the Tropic . . .' He compressed his lips for a moment before he went on to add, 'But we still have Garland to worry about.'

'What does your policeman friend suggest?' asked Simon. 'I've left a message on the boss's answerphone—can't do any more until he rings back.'

'He says we should hang about near the restaurant, in case we spot a familiar figure. If we do, he suggests we keep an eye on where they go—discreetly, of course—but we must not approach them until he joins us here. Meanwhile, he's putting the villa under surveillance.'

Simon uttered a sigh of relief. 'Well, that sounds more promising. Did he have anything else to say?'

Nic nodded, his expression grave. 'Yes, he's the one who was called in to attend my accident and he told me they have uncovered more on the racket in which Sarah had become involved.'

'So you were right, there is something going on, but why had Sarah left the villa? I would have thought she'd have waited once she informed the police.'

'Actually, Sarah is quite naïve. Evidently, she did not realise she had been doing anything illegal until her hairdresser happened to make a chance remark when she called at the salon last week . . .'

'Illegal, you say?' Simon broke in. 'My boss wouldn't like that.'

'Yes. From what I have heard, it seems the hairdresser had complimented Sarah on a particular dress she was wearing when, on her return from a visit to France the previous evening, she had spotted Sarah taking charge of a Four by Four somewhere near the border.'

'But why on earth would Sarah want to drive something like that?'

'Ah, but it was not Sarah. When the hairdresser commented on the colour and design of the dress, and sympathised with Sarah over the problem of climbing into such a vehicle wearing an extremely slim skirt, Sarah was puzzled. But on further description she recognised it as being one of the stylish outfits she had seen her friend Patricia wearing.'

'So Sarah's friend was driving illegally, you mean? They must look very much alike for her own hairdresser to make such a mistake.'

'In height and hair colour, I suppose they are,' Nic agreed, keeping an eye on the people passing by. 'But it doesn't end there, according to my friend it was on her return to the villa when the trouble started. Evidently, Sarah discovered a Four by Four in the garage, but finding the engine was cold she guessed it had been there since early morning, or possibly overnight. I understand she became suspicious of its origins and challenged the Blanford woman about how the vehicle came to be in her garage. But the woman then told her she was already involved by having stored similar vehicles, and reminded her it had been for a considerable sum of money.'

'If she did, then she couldn't really complain,' Simon commented with a short laugh as they turned to stroll back along the busy narrow street.

'Ah yes, but only after it had occurred to her that an unusual number of cars were being moved did she voice her suspicions and object to being involved. As a result, she was threatcned and because of that she became extremely nervous, even frightened, and decided to get away and inform . . .' He broke off and gripped Simon's arm, drawing him to a halt. And his heart lurched as he said softly, 'Over there, going into the restaurant—it is the same man.'

Simon's eyes widened. 'You're right! But where's your police officer?'

Nic kept a surreptitious eye on thc business opposite as he spoke. 'He will be here, but if our target comes out of the restaurant, I'll follow him.'

'I thought you said the officer advised us not to approach him.'

'Don't worry, much as I would like to, I'll resist, but at least I shall know where he resides.'

*   *   *

'Damned answerphone!' Don muttered to himself in disgust and thrust his mobile into his pocket. He was beginning to wish he hadn't sent Patricia and Juan to move the car until Gomez was back and he'd been in touch with McLeod. He glanced towards the kitchen where Garland waited and listened, hoping he'd be rid of this diabetic woman in a good state of health, and the sooner the better. He was feeling slightly nervous, wondering what was keeping Gomez so long? He had done nothing but complain . . .'

Hearing the sound of feet on the stone steps leading up from the main entrance he gave a heavy sigh of impatience and moved towards the hall door as Garland sprang to her feet and hurried across the kitchen, seeking an escape.

There was a crash as the door burst open, but it wasn't Gomez or Sarah who entered. Instead, a number of uniformed men rushed in, filling the hall.

'*Senorita* McLeod?' enquired another man

152

who was wearing civilian clothes. Observing her expression of alarm he gave her a brief smile and explained, 'I am the police. You are safe now.'

Garland could only nod as tears of relief filled her eyes, blurring her vision so that she could not clearly make out the defeated figure of Don as he was being hustled past. She could hear a mixture of raised voices in both English and Spanish, but could only define Don's wail of protest as he was taken from the building, shouting, 'Don't think your sister will get away with this!'

She felt the policeman's hand beneath her elbow, urging her to take a seat whilst she recovered. Then she heard Nic's voice and his hurried footsteps and she quickly rose to her feet again with a cry of relief.

'Garland!' cried Nic. 'Are you all right, darling? They haven't hurt you, have they?' And he gently enfolded her in his arms.

Sobbing against the soft fabric of Nic's jacket, she managed to gasp an assurance that she was quite unharmed. And as he wiped away her tears she met the concerned expression on Simon's face as he hovered a little self-consciously nearby.

'How did you f-find m-me?' she stammered. 'Have you seen Sarah?'

Turning towards the man in plain clothes Nic said, 'Don't worry, she's safe, as my friend here will tell you.'

'I'm sure she hasn't done anything wrong,' Garland said brokenly, 'not intentionally, I mean . . .'

'No no, *senorita*, is no problem,' said the policeman with a comforting smile. He then went on to relate how Sarah's information had led them to the vehicle which she had driven away from the villa, and the garage where it was intended to go for the necessary adjustments to its ownership.

'Sarah had been threatened, if she didn't deliver the vehicle there would be trouble. Naturally, she was frightened which is why she left the villa and drove the Four by Four to a place where the police could find it,' Nic supplied when he saw Garland's puzzled expression. 'Then she went to a nearby hotel to pass on the information and keep watch rather than risk being found at the villa.'

'And where is she now?' asked Garland. 'I'd like to see her as soon as I can. Meredith was hoping to hold us both to ransom and bring my father over to pay but he only got the answerphone when he rang.' Her expression became sad as she continued, 'Pity really, now I know Sarah's safe it could have been an ideal opportunity to get them together.'

'No problem there,' Simon interjected, 'your father is already on his way. Fortunately, I just caught him as he arrived home from business, and he said he was setting off for the airport immediately.'

Fresh tears welled in Garland's eyes but this time they were not only those of relief. 'I hope we can go back to the villa now,' she said then, noticing a uniformed man standing in the entrance, asked, 'Where have you taken them—we don't have to stay here do we?'

'Don't worry, those three will not be getting up to any more tricks for a while,' Simon grinned. 'You know, your father never did trust Meredith, or the Blanford woman.'

'But what about the other man, Gomez? He'd gone to wait for Sarah . . .'

Nic laughed. 'We met him on the street, bringing his meal back here.'

'Oh yes, I had a meal brought in from that restaurant we visited,' she told him, managing a smile.

'And did you have snails?' he asked with unsuppressed amusement. 'You know, your artistic skills provided a valuable clue.'

The plain-clothes officer then gave instructions for the apartment to be searched, and to Nic he said, 'We will drive the *senorita* back to the villa to await the arrival of her father. I have a few questions I wish to put to her sister which I prefer to complete tonight.'

Garland looked at Nic. 'But what about you and Simon?' she asked. 'You both have a busy day ahead of you.'

'After a good night's rest we will be back on the course in the morning.' he assured her and whispered. 'Sleep well, my darling, I'll ring you tomorrow.'

*   *   *

When he saw Sarah's state of distress, the policeman who drove Garland back to the villa decided against putting further questions to her that evening and stated his intention to return the following day.

Over a relaxing drink, Garland listened patiently until Sarah had exhausted the topic of Don Meredith and Patricia Blanford and their wicked ways. It surprised her to see how vulnerable her sister was beneath her usual well-groomed confidence. Instead she saw an anxious and sensitive woman who appeared woefully insecure. But now that Sarah had opened her heart, Garland sensibly made no comment on her stupidity and merely allowed her to ramble on until she heard the sound of a vehicle drawing up outside.

As James McLeod alighted from the taxi that had brought him from the airport, Sarah rushed out to welcome him, bringing a lump to Garland's throat as she followed her down the path.

'Ach no, let's not have tears, you're supposed to be pleased to see me!' her father exclaimed laughingly as he hugged Sarah to him.

'It's just that I'm so pleased you're here . . .' she said brokenly.

156

'And this is how it is going to be from now on,' her father declared happily, his arms round both his daughters. 'I'm going to enjoy being here with you both this weekend.'

'The police will be calling tomorrow,' Garland said, 'and I suppose I shall have to join Simon at the tournament.'

'There's no need for you to go as I intend going over to the course myself,' James declared as he withdrew the cork from a bottle of wine. 'I'm rather proud of you, and young Simon . . . and you, Sarah,' he added quickly. 'It would take courage to speak up against those two and their thieving racket.'

Seeing Sarah's ready tears, Garland took the glass of wine he offered and to change the subject, said lightly, 'Simon will be pleased, he's worked hard.'

James realized what Garland was about, said, 'He rang me only this morning to give me the figures, and I'm delighted over the success of our new lines, and the amount of orders taken.' He paused a moment and grinned at her, then said, 'And what's this I hear about you and Nic Maragall?'

*   *   *

The following day after the policeman had completed his questioning, Garland and Sarah relaxed on the patio with increasing friendliness. And when Mark Thomson

157

entered the conversation Sarah was surprised to learn that Garland was already aware of his intended visit the following day.

'I was worried, and I couldn't contact you so I rang him,' Garland told her.

'Oh I'm sorry, Sis. I've been such a pain causing you so much trouble.'

'Never mind that, Sarah, there won't be any charges so it's behind you now. And you have Mark's visit to look forward to, I'm so pleased about that.'

'So am I,' said Sarah with a contented sigh. 'I want to make up for my beastly treatment of him last year.'

'I hope everything works out well for you, Sarah.'

'And you,' Sarah said with a smile. 'I believe I was rather nasty about that man from the Tropic. I'm sure he's very nice and I hope you'll forgive me.'

'Of course I'll forgive you, and yes, he is very nice,' said Garland, smiling to herself as she remembered the sensations Nic's kisses had evoked, her love for him causing her to ache with longing to be enfolded in his arms.

That evening Simon telephoned her at the villa, using James's mobile. 'We have had a great day!' he said, enthusiastic as usual.

'Have you seen Nic?' she asked, slightly peeved because he hadn't called.

'Since play finished, he's been rather busy with the police regarding his accident. He'll probably ring you later.'

'Thanks, Simon. All being well, I'll see you in the morning.'

'Not sure, I think your father is staying on for the rest of the tournament,' he told her. 'Anyhow, I'll see you in Scotland.'

Nic didn't ring her that evening, even though the telephone had been reconnected, and it was after lunch the following day when Garland received his brief call enquiring if she was all right after her experiences.

'Wish me luck, Garland,' he said softly.

'Yes, of course,' she responded delightedly.

'I hope I shall see you before you leave for home?'

'I hope so too,' she said, though her heart was heavy at the thought of it.

'Even if I lose?'

Garland smiled. 'Oh yes, Nic, win or lose . . .' she agreed breathlessly.

The screaming note of a jet engine sounded overhead as a plane flew low in preparation for landing at the nearby airport, reminding her that time here was getting short and Nic had not made a firm arrangement to meet.

*   *   *

'Don't you think you ought to call on Pedro?' asked Sarah with more than usual concern. 'After all, you're leaving early the day after tomorrow.'

'I'll have time in the morning,' Garland replied without enthusiasm.

'But Mark will be here in the morning, I thought you'd want to meet him.'

'Yes, of course I do,' Garland said and glanced at her watch. 'All right, I'll go, though I'm a bit later than usual. But if anyone rings . . .'

'Don't worry I'll take a message,' Sarah broke in to assure her, adding with an encouraging smile. 'No need to rush, Pops won't be back for some time.'

The little town was bathed in sunshine when Garland walked down to the promenade. Her heart was heavy—she'd had no word from Nic suggesting a time to meet—was he avoiding her she wondered sadly? Arriving at the café she selected the table on the patio where she and Nic had dinner a few evenings ago, but she chose to sit with her back towards the Tropic Hotel as the memories began to crowd in. Perhaps it was foolish to have come here when she could have paid a brief call on Pedro on her way to the airport.

To Pedro's usual enquiring smile from the doorway she nodded. But, minutes later, expecting to be served lemon tea she gave him a puzzled look when he set down his tray bearing a bottle of sparkling wine and two glasses.

'Are you joining me in a farewell drink?' she asked.

But Pedro merely cast her a mysterious smile and proceeded to open the bottle and pour the bubbling wine into the glasses, retreating when a voice behind asked, 'May I join you?' and her heart leapt as she turned to see Nic standing there.

'You are a little later than usual, thank goodness,' he said, stooping to kiss her cheek. 'I didn't think I'd get here in time.'

'My farewell drink,' she said with a heavy heart.

'No, Garland, not farewell, just a toast to the years ahead of us.'

She looked at him, mystified. 'Us? I don't understand . . .'

'Then tell me, what made you choose this table,' he asked, and saw her cheeks grow faintly pink. 'Dare I hope it was for sentimental reasons?'

'Oh, Nic, I didn't think I would see you again,' she said, tears brimming.

'You'll not get rid of me so easily,' he laughed. 'I would like us to make our friendship permanent.'

'Permanent?' she whispered as he clinked his glass against hers.

'Yes . . . that is, if you will have me.' Taking a golf ball from his pocket, he said, 'It is usual for the winner to throw it to the crowd but I kept it for you—you brought me luck. I love you, Garland,' he murmured, taking her hand. 'I want you to be my wife.'